DARK YONDER

Tales & Tabs

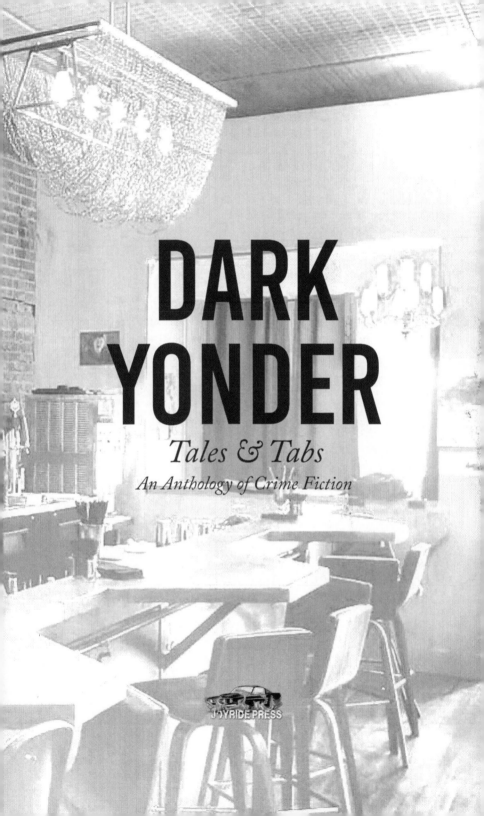

DARK
YONDER

Tales & Tabs

An Anthology of Crime Fiction

JOYRIDE PRESS

Joyride Press
P.O. Box 153
Troy, NY 12182

Printed in the United States of America.

ISBN: 978-0-9908669-2-3

DEDICATION

This anthology is dedicated to Yonder: Southern Cocktails & Brew, a place of magic and mayhem. May it never actually see the characters that grace its doors within these pages. And to everyone in search of a good cocktail.

COCKTAIL MENU

Introduction, by Eryk Pruitt – 9

Hey Barkeep! By Eryk Pruitt – 13

A True Yonder Tale, by Dan Barbour – 17

Them's Fighting Words, by Travis Richardson – 23

Run Its Course, by Frank Zafiro – 35

Popcorn, by Gabriel Valjan – 49

Living Proof, by Will Viharo – 63

Off-Label, by Terri Lynn Coop – 77

Yonder There's a Margarita, by Matt Phillips – 89

The Regular, by Eric Beetner – 103

Slappy Sacramento, by Todd Morr – 113

Huey and the Burrito of Doom, by Nick Kolakowski – 123

The Door in the Floor, by Allison Davis – 135

Close Your Laptop, by Judy Wilkinson – 145

They Have Drinks Named After Famous Writers, by S.A. Cosby – 153

Legs Diamond, by Liam Sweeny – 165

The Proposition, by Philip Kimbrough – 177

Llama Juice, by Stacie A. Leininger – 187

Moist Money, by Greg Herren – 199

Old Fashioned, by Bruce Robert Coffin – 213

The Big Splash, by Renato Bratkovič – 223

Noir at the Bar Fight, by Dana King – 235

Two Clowns Walk into a Bar, by Jim Shaffer – 249

Retribution, by David Nemeth – 265

Not Enough to Drink, by Rob Pierce – 279

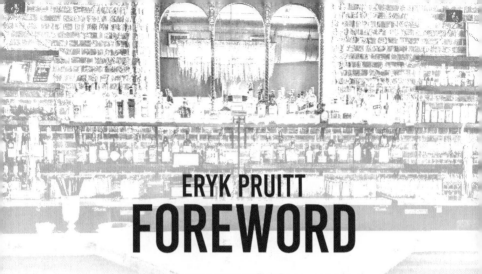

FOREWORD

How y'all are?

Welcome to Yonder, where we serve fine, handcrafted Southern cocktails and local brews to the upstanding patrons of beautiful, downtown, colonial AF Hillsborough, North Carolina.

Sign the membership log, then grab a stool.

Settle in for a story or two.

Can't make it to Yonder? No problem! Liam Sweeny devised a way to get a slice of Yonder to all the folks not privileged to live within crawling distance of King Street.

Hence, Dark Yonder.

Inside, you'll find several of the cocktails Lana and I have featured at Yonder, along with the many quotes that accompanied them on our menu. You won't find any measurements, because I'm Southern as a copperhead and can't be bothered with such foofooraw. Need to make a drink less strong? Just add ginger beer…

You'll also find some hard-hitting tales written by some of the best crime fiction authors working today. Gabriel Valjan gives Yonder serious street cred when an infamous moonshiner stops by to pay a call. Shawn A. Cosby honors our bar with a visit from the most terrifying character from his crime-ridden canon. Vic Valentine darkens our doors, thanks to the great Will Viharo.

You'll find exceptionally great stories, like Judy Wilkinson's "Close Your Laptop," which I've had the pleasure of seeing her read live at Yonder's many *Noir at the Bar* events. Or Todd Morr's "Sloppy Sacramento" which will give me pause before I call anyone a dummy ever again. Watch for Dana King's near-nonfiction turn with "Noir at the Bar Fight." And for god's sake DO NOT SLEEP on Greg Herren's "Moist Money." That guy...

You'll find more than one crack about the way I spell my name...

You know what you won't find?

PBR.

Nary a bottle or can of it.

We care too much about our customers to let them drink that shit.

We're old school bartenders here. We know making a drink is only half of the job. When we slip the bar towel and the church key in our back pocket, the curtains have lifted. The lights may be dim, but it's our job to entertain. Or fade into the background. It's our job to listen to how your day is going. We're supposed to be quick with a joke.

Or a story.

I've met people who have never been fired from a job. I'm not one of them. I've been fired from dozens upon dozens of jobs throughout my entire life. How else would I know it's time to stop working there? For years, I've gotten dressed for work wondering if it was all for naught, if this was the night my employment would suddenly terminate.

These days when I get dressed for work, I appreciate that, for the first time in my life, I can't be fired.

I can totally go to prison, though.

Three times per shift I look at something and say "I could be incarcerated for that."

Thankfully Lana is there to help keep me straight. None of this could be done without her, and you'll find plenty of anecdotes about her as well. The bar would be awfully dark if it weren't for the reigning Employee of the Month making sure the light bill was paid.

It doesn't matter if you live five miles or five-hundred miles away. Thanks to Liam Sweeney and this wonderful crew of regulars, you can always have a home at Yonder.

Eryk Pruitt

ERYK PRUITT

HEY BARKEEP, YOU'D BE A LOT PRETTIER IF YOU SMILED

Hey look, I get it: You're way too busy working on your novel/album/app/collection of nouveau beat poetry criticisms, but I'm getting parched over here. I could use a drink. Especially after the past ten minutes, flagging you down, stuck listening to your shitty music which, by the way, sounds like a cross between Yoko Ono and a hipster castoff from America's Got Talent. There's a reason why they're obscure, dude.

I know, I know…If you wrote a book titled Fifty Things I'd Rather Do Than Make This Guy A Drink, it would probably be a long one and would include such compelling chapters as "Instagramming My Inventive Facial Hair #HandlebarStache, #LumberJackBeard" or "Sculpting the Perfect Ball of Ice with a Only a Pick and Sheer Determination." However, since you can only make one drink at a time, we better get started or I'll be here until Last Call.

I don't know when it happened, but some (not all!) bartenders have become total pricks when it comes to making drinks. It was troubling enough when the New Age got old enough to drink, but now they're old enough to pour booze and they've single-handedly wrecked the social scene. Instead of customer service, a handful of rotten apples place priority on smashing herbs, adding bitters, and employing a complicated system of weights and measures. Last thing I need when I'm thirsty is to be pushed around by some snowflake in a bowtie.

I can see it takes you ten minutes to hand craft a cocktail, but you're in luck! Anything more than ice in my liquor and I get the fidgets, so why not save the foofooraw for someone who appreciates it? And yes—don't roll your eyes—I want ice in my bourbon. I know damn well it's Maker's Mark, because I'm the one paying for it. The war's over; give me more ice cubes. And I don't need you muttering under your breath, telling me how to drink my booze, you bougie douche. If I'm paying $12 per ounce, I'll take it how I goddamn want.

Now, wait…I did not mean to get off on the wrong foot. The last thing I want is to give cause for your snotty attitude. It's just that I came up in a different age—old school, if you will—where we practiced words like hospitality (look it up) and bars were a fun place to hang out. Back then, you learned all you needed to know about bartending by watching a battered VHS copy of Cocktail (ask your parents). So pardon me if I get a bit chapped to see that you've put more effort into your costume (Arm garters? Really?) than you have with witty banter. Forgive my shock and awe that you eschewed a warm, friendly greeting for twenty extra flavors of bitters and a penchant for Kabuki.

The world doesn't need another person taking themselves too serious. What it needs is a drink. A joke. Those are things you can look up on your phone, if needed. However, you can Google neither a warm personality nor a sense of urgency, both of which you're going to need if you expect me to sit in your cranky old bar, waiting for you to make me a drink.

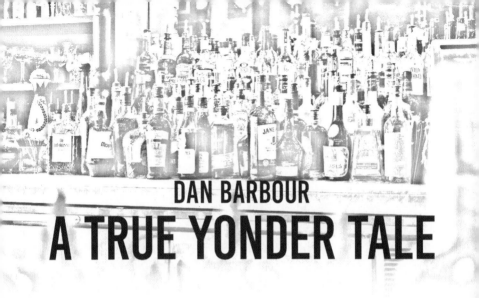

DAN BARBOUR
A TRUE YONDER TALE

I was working when I received a call from Sharon, a new friend
that had seen our band, The Ellerbe Creek Band, play at Bright-
leaf one weekend. She said there was a new bar in Hillsborough
that was under new management and was looking to start up a music
scene. "I told them they need to get you guys in there. Call up and
talk to Eryk." I called Eryk that day and we worked out a date for
a Saturday evening not too far in the future for us to play for a few
hours.

The day approached and our excitement of getting to play a new
location increased. We were performing acoustically, which was a
fun change from the normal full electric with lights and all. Now for
most musicians, an acoustic gig means less equipment to carry in. As
the bass player, not for me. We were going to play without a drum-
mer, which meant I was going to have to perform the percussion as
well. This means I will have a foot tambourine on my right foot and
will be tapping on a stomp box with my left foot. The stomp box
has an electric pick up in it that sounds like a bass drum when tapped,
so I have to bring a separate amp as well as my bass amp just for this
feature. And since I have to sit down to do this I have to bring my
stool also. Usually by the end of the night I will have walked many
miles after stepping from foot to foot keeping the beat going for the

group. It's pretty tiring, but totally worth it.

The night started with us loading in and I finally get to meet Eryk, the man behind the voice on the phone. We set up and we started to get a nice crowd filling in. It's always fun to play for people who have never seen or heard your band, we always gather new friends and fans every time. The first set went really well and people seemed to be enjoying the show. After the set I was walking around, introducing myself to anyone who wanted to chat and met some members of another band that were scheduled to play here in a couple of weeks. They seemed pretty excited about it after seeing the bar and the patrons that were there.

As we started the second set, I sat on my stool and started to have a pain on the right side of my body, felt like a cramp. Being 44 I shook it off and continued stomping, tapping, and singing for the next 2 hours. After the show was over and all the gear was loaded up I hung around a little while with our singer and we had a beer and chatted with Eryk about how we really enjoyed playing at the new place and all the great people we met. As I headed home the pain started to set in a bit more and I thought to myself "Just get home, get some rest. It'll probably be gone in the morning."

By Sunday evening I was curled up in the fetal position on my bed shaking like I was freezing, crying out in pain. I assumed from stories I've heard it was a kidney stone. After a trip to the ER And some scans I was shocked to learn that my appendix had ruptured and would need emergency surgery due to the fact that the infection and inflammation had obstructed my bowels. I had to have some of my small and large intestine removed and had a very long incision that took over 20 staples to close. I spent the next 3 weeks in the hospital in recovery.

After I was released from the hospital I had spoken with Eryk and rebooked our band to play a second time in June. It was far enough away that I would have the chance to fully recover. This would be my return to the scene where it all went down. Then Eryk contacted me and told me that he was taking part ownership of the bar and apologized that unfortunately our show would have rescheduled. I was thrilled for him, but saddened that I would have to wait to make my return. I then learned that "Yonder" would be the new name, seemed appropriate for the small town atmosphere that Hillsborough has. After juggling the schedules of the other band members and other shows we had already booked, we were able to work out a date, August 24th, dangling the carrot in front of me just a while longer.

Dan Barbour

Bassist (and part time percussion) for The Ellerbe Creek Band

SUFFERING BASTARD

Bourbon
Gin
Angostura
Lime
Ginger Beer

"Too much of anything is bad, but too much good whiskey is barely enough."
– Mark Twain

Amounts have been left out. Live a little.

THEM'S FIGHTING WORDS

G rady Edwards sat back in his La-Z-Boy with a bottle of Bud Light in one hand and a remote in the other, flipping between reality shows about moonshining, Okie noodling (aka cat-fishing by hand), and competitive hog calling. All redneck reality shows that proved to the rest of America and world that people like him were fools because they were poor and had an accent. The pro-grams both repulsed and fascinated him, and goldarnit if there wasn't a shred of truth in all that exaggerated reality. The doorbell rang, and Grady wondered who the hell would be bothering him. He pushed his six foot four frame out of the chair and lumbered to the door, kicking cans and other crap out of his way. He wasn't sure when it happened, but once he moved north of thirty, things just seemed to move a little slower. Stupid aches that didn't do anybody any good seemed to be more constant than any woman in his life, that was for certain. Whoever was interrupting his quality time had better have something good to say or at least some booze, ass, or grass.

Opening the door, two men stood in front of him. Strangers. Both men were solid, about his height and build with scruffy beards. One wore glasses. He felt suspicious about that one.

"Who are you?"

The one without glasses, a dude with spiked sandy hair stepped forward with an outstretched hand and a natural smile.

"Hey there. My name's Eryk Pruitt, and this here is my partner, Drew." Grady couldn't help but shake Eryk's hand. "We're out here doing an investigative report on the unsolved murder of Jessica Talbert. Would you be willin' to talk to us for a few minutes?"

Grady heard about these fellas snoopin' around Pinewood Hollow the last couple of days askin' questions nobody wanted to answer. Should've figured they'd wind up on his doorstep sooner or later. "They arrested that black fella back in the day for it. Don't see why you're here now."

"I guess you haven't heard that DNA exonerated Wesley Winston of all charges. They released him, and he's gettin' a few million in compensation from the state now."

Grady shook his head and spat. "Lucky coon. Don't they always get everything for free from the government?"

He expected that knowing nod he usually gets from his neighbors when he says anything about minorities, women, or Democrats. Instead Eryk and his partner shared a look like he farted in church or something.

"Wesley did serve over twenty years for a crime he didn't commit," Eryk said. "There's probably some compensation due to him, don't you think? Especially considerin' he didn't do it. It was even documented he was in another county the entire weekend the murder happened. Not that a jury cared."

"Yeah, well, he still got free housin', food, and cable during that time. You wanna see how much my cable bill is? I can't feel like he got that bad of a deal."

Of course, deep inside he knew Wesley got a raw deal, regardless of his race, but the guy who murdered that teenage girl was his uncle. She'd been one of them girls who bloomed a little too quickly and got his Uncle Meryl's sights. Certain folks around here knew that. But out here in the sticks, kin don't rat on kin or their neighbors. And what the hell was he doing wasting his time with these assholes when he was missing out on whether Jimbo had finally caught the seventy-pound cat he'd been dreaming of pulling out of that lake.

"We know you probably weren't the one to have—" the other man started to say, but Grady had had enough.

"Get off my porch or I'll bring out my buddies Smith and Wesson to get your asses outta here."

And that was that. He slammed the door in their faces and got back to the La-Z-Boy in time to see Jimbo noodle out a disappointing forty-pound cat. His dreams fell short, like just about everybody he knew around here.

★★★

Those two guys snooped around Pinewood Hollow for another week before they disappeared to everybody's relief. A bunch of troublemakers asking questions nobody wanted to answer. Was a time when folks would run outsiders like that out on a rail or maybe take them on a long walk into the woods and make sure they never came back out. Can't do none of that no more, Grady lamented. So much for the good old days. Anyway, things were pretty much back to normal for a couple of months until the state police showed up on Uncle Meryl's porch and arrested him. News about what he'd done went far and wide. News vans from Raleigh and Charlottesville and other places drove up and tried to get more people to talk. Most folks either acted shocked or ignored them. Ended up that those two asshole reporters had found enough clues to link the murder to Grady's uncle, and then they stole a fork from a barbeque joint that Uncle Meryl frequented. They were lauded as heroes, not petty thieves. That burned Grady something awful. Ain't that a prime example of how the liberal media works.

Another month or two passed, and everybody around town ended up being okay with Uncle Meryl going to jail. Actually they were somewhat relieved and openly admitted he'd always been an asshole with a quick temper. Grady had seen his cousins get whipped mightily over the slightest offenses. And personally, Grady felt like a load had slid off his shoulders not carrying around that dark secret any-

25

more. Everything seemed to be back to normal, and then he heard that damn podcast.

The Long Dance 2: Secrets of Pinewood Hollow. Dang. Those fellas were tenacious and then some on their journey to take down his uncle. They did all sorts of research. Interviewing Wesley Winston and his family first. And holy hell if it wasn't hard not to shed a tear for him, even if he was black and a millionaire.

Then the victim's family talked in the next episode. The Talberts moved to Durham five years after Jessica's death. At first, they had a hard time believing it wasn't Wesley. They'd spent the last twenty years fixated on hating one man it was hard for them to do much else, let alone figure it might be somebody different. Even with DNA, they countered that you can't really believe scientists because they get things wrong all the time. Grady couldn't agree more, but if he didn't know better, they sounded a bit like the OJ Simpson jury from the mid-nineties…with stronger accents. When Eryk asked the family if they'd be satisfied to continue blaming an acquitted man when there was the very real possibility that the murderer of their beloved girl might still be alive and enjoying twenty plus years of freedom without one ounce of justice ever served against him, that got them quieted for a bit. Eventually they jumped ship, believing Wesley had been falsely convicted and that the real murderer had lived amongst them when they lived back in Pinewood Hollow.

Those were the first three episodes. Episode four was something different entirely. That's when Eryk and Drew drove out to Pinewood Hollow. Grady had started to take a sip of his third Bud Light when he heard his own voice over the computer speakers.

"Get off my porch or I'll bring out my buddies Smith and Wesson to get your asses outta here."

Eryk's voice followed. "Yep, that was pretty much the reception we got on the other side of the tracks in Pinewood Hollow, but none was as elegant and sophisticated as the man you heard there, Grady Edwards, nephew of Meryl Edwards. A self-righteous, second-amendment-loving scholar who seemed more interested in beer than employment if one were to judge by his breath and general state of hygiene."

Grady spit out his beer and lifted himself out of the La-Z-Boy. He didn't quite understand everything that Eryk said, but he knew one thing. Eryk just got himself a beat down. He done called him out all over the country or maybe the world (although he wasn't sure exactly how podcasts worked). Since Grady didn't have his own podcast, there was only one way to answer back, and it didn't involve fancy pants words. Just his right and left fists and a steel-toed boot.

It didn't take Grady long to find out that Eryk co-owned a bar called Yonder over in Hillsborough, near Durham. A two and half hour drive on the I-85. It was already after nine PM, so he oughta get there before midnight. After a night of slinging booze, that smart talkin', funny first name spellin' Eryk fellow would get to know the real meaning of closing time.

Grady laughed to himself as he walked out the door and threw an aluminum baseball bat into the back of his F-150 beater.

"Unemployed, my ass," Grady mumbled as he got behind the wheel and started the truck up with a belch of smoke. "After I give Eryk an asswhippin' I might start up a career in stand-up comedy."

★★★

It was another busy night at the Yonder Southern Cocktails and Brew. Not as busy as say Noir at the Bar or Jell-O-Sumo Wrestling night, but Eryk and his wife, Lana Pierce, didn't seem to stop pouring and mixing for most of the evening. And it was a Wednesday night. The success of nailing that scumbag Meryl Edwards had really raised the bar's profile.

Then in midst of serving the masses, disaster struck. They ran out of bitters. Any self-respecting person living below the Mason-Dixon Line knows you can't make an authentic Southern old-fashion without bitters. Want a Sazerac? Good luck without it. Might as well call this place Yonder Brews and Random Drinks. This was worse than the time they ran out of grenadine on a sweltering Saturday a few months back. Alabama Slammers and Carolina Hurricanes had to be put on hold until more of that sweet and tart red sauce could be scrounged up, much to the chagrin of a group of Millennials. Lana ran out to pick up more from a supplier in Durham who stayed open late for these kinds of emergencies.

A couple of regulars called it a night and Eryk wished them well as he began to wipe down the far end of the bar. A few seconds later, the front door opened with a crash. He looked up to see some dude, big and familiar, march in like he had a bone to pick. Or bash as he held an unmistakable bat in his hand. Eryk then realized who he was.

"Hey there, Grady. Long time no see. How's your uncle doin'?"

The man's stride halted as his face twisted for a second. He had had something on his mind. A line to deliver or something of rehearsed importance, but Eryk's question threw him out of sync.

"He's just fine, considerin'." He shook his head and took another step forward.

Eryk used that pause to position himself behind an open shelf under the bar where a loaded Sig Sauer resided. He cracked a smile. "I bet. Enjoyin' the free meals, cable, and lathering up in communal spaces. What's not to love? Other people do his laundry too, I bet. He's livin' high on the hog."

Grady's mouth hung open, his movement bogged down with hesitation. He pointed a finger at Eryk. "Look here. No more jibber-jabberin'. I want you to come outside where we can settle some unfinished business."

"You wanna drink first? Comin' all the way over from Pinewood Hollow, I imagine you're mighty thirsty."

"Naw, I'd rather get this done now." But the man's hungry eyes, scrutinizing the whiskeys on the shelf, told a different story.

"Do I need to bring a sidearm?"

Grady looked at his bat. "I just brought this here bat. My plan is to open a can of whup ass on you. If you wanna shootout, I'll go get a rifle outta my truck."

Eryk shooed him away with his hand. "No need to do that. We'll settle this man to man. With the fists or blunt objects if you really need 'em."

By this point all of the patrons had stopped their discussions and watched the two men.

"You need some help, Eryk?" one of them asked.

Eryk took a belt of Jack and came around the bar. "Naw, I got it. We're just steppin' outside to have ourselves a little conversation. I shan't be long."

On his way out the door, Grady flipped a table over and glanced back at Eryk with raised eyebrows. Eryk felt blood rise to his face, but he knew he had to keep his emotions in check. He was going to kick this racist, nephew-of-a-murderer's butt and then some. First he needed to disarm him of that pesky Louisville Slugger, then he'd open his own can of whup ass.

Walking outside into the still humid North Carolina air, Eryk thought about inviting the dipshit back inside to duke it out in the A/C. Sure, they might break a few tables, but not as much sweat. He rolled up his sleeves instead. Patrons walked outside to watch the showdown on the sidewalk.

"I wanna say you're a low down dirty son of a bitch comin' up with all those lies and—" Grady started to say.

"And you covered up for your uncle who violently raped and murdered a teenage girl."

Grady stood with his mouth wide open. "How did you—"

"Your cousin Jolene told me off the record that you knew. Saw her get in his truck." Eryk shook his head. "That's down right awful, man, letting that uncle of yours carry on with all that blood on his hands."

Grady licked his lips. "Well, he had some issues, but he's in prison now. Ain't he?"

"After another man served twenty years—"

"But he's sittin' pretty now, huh?"

"There's two decades of life he never lived thanks to you and your kin coverin' up."

"Well, forget about all that. I'm here because of what you said on that dance long podcast of yours or whatever it's called."

"The Long Dance," Liam, a regular, shouted.

"Yeah, whatever. Stupid name anyhow. But when you called me"—Grady threw up his hands and did air quotes with his fingers—"an unemployed beer drinker with bad breath. You crossed a line buddy."

"That's not what I said. It was something like you're—and I quote—more interested in beer than employment if one were to judge by his breath and general state of hygiene. End quote."

The crowd laughed. Grady shook with rage.

"Them's fightin' words, Eryk Pruitt."

"Yet," Eryk said with one eyebrow arched higher than the other. "All of them words are absolutely true."

Grady's eyes widened as he lifted the bat to shoulder. Eryk wasted no time, rushing the knucklehead and plowing into his beer gut before he could bring the bat down. He slammed his back against a tall concrete planter. The bat fell from Grady's hands with a clang and rolled out on to the street. Eryk stepped back and brought a right uppercut to the breathless man's jaw. He teetered. Eryk finished him with a left hook to his right eye. Grady's legs twisted as he crumpled to the pavement. Eryk shook the left hand, the knuckles aching something fierce.

"Fuckin' hard headed bastard."

The crowd laughed again and patted Eryk on the back.

"Let's go back inside where it's cooler. Drinks are on da house."

Everybody cheered.

"Eryk, watch out!" Liam shouted.

He turned to see Grady pick himself up and pull a small semi-automatic from the back of his jeans.

Eryk raised his hands in the air. "Whoa, man, you said you weren't armed. What's up with that?"

"Yeah, well. I guess you're the stupid one now." Grady gave a triumphant smile through his bloody lips.

A clang resounded through the street as Grady crossed his eyes and fell to the ground on his face. Lana stood above the unconscious body, the Slugger gripped firmly in her hands.

"Hey there, darling," Eryk said with a smile of relief. "You just hit one humdinger of a home run."

His wife put the bat up to her shoulder. "And you couldn't resolve this situation by talking?"

Eryk shook his head. "Nu-uh. Not in the least. He wanted nothing less than a to fight. Come on, back me up, fellas."

The crowd nodded and murmured yes, but didn't look at Lana.

"And you couldn't call the police?"

"I didn't know there'd be guns involved, honey. That lyin' bastard told me as much."

"Uh huh." She tossed the bat to the ground. Eryk sighed, letting his shoulders relax. "Next time you knock a man to the ground, you best make sure he stays down. You hear me, honey?"

"Clear as moonshine."

"Well, let's not keep these good folks waiting any longer. One round on the house."

The patrons cheered as they made their way inside the building. Lana placed a firm kiss on Eryk's lips.

"You had a couple good swings in there yourself," she said.

"Wait, you were watchin' me?"

"Just waiting to see how long it'd take before you needed back up."

"You know I can't do anything without you, honey."

"Quit preachin' to the choir." She slapped Eryk on the behind. "Get on in there and serve those thirsty customers."

Eryk went to the door, stopped, and gave her one more kiss. Hot damn, he was one lucky guy.

Edited by Liam Sweeny

SWEET TEA MINT JULEP

Bourbon
Mint
Sugar
Southern Sweet Tea

*"Death is one moment, and life is so
many of them."*
– Tennessee Williams

Amounts have been left out. Live a little.

FRANK ZAFIRO
RUN ITS COURSE

When she came in the bar, it was clear she wanted to be alone.

The message was etched into every aspect of her being. The dark, taut expression of her face. The purposeful stride. The way her eyes swept the inside of the Yonder to take in the scene, but didn't linger on anything. Or anyone.

At the bar, she remained standing. Eryk sauntered over, leaning in to take her order. Like any good bartender, he seemed to sense her mood and let her be. He poured her a shot and pulled a light beer from the tap, a combination that meant business. She took both and made her way to a small table along the wall on the other side of the room.

I watched all of this from my seat at the end of the bar.

Her name was Alana. I knew this because we'd had a few short conversations over the past week. Usually, she came in with the people she worked with, so our talks didn't last long. But I liked her. She had spirit. And I think she liked me.

I waited a bit, finishing up my drink. After Eryk poured me another, I picked up my glass and walked over to Alana's table. Ever the cop, she spotted me before I even got close. I watched her eyes for a dismissal, but all I saw there was something broken and hollow.

I sat. Alana's shot was only half gone. Same with the beer. So much for meaning business.

"Drinking alone?" I ventured.

She shrugged.

"I figure I could be a detective," I said, "what with how great I am at picking out details."

She let out a tiny snort that was meant to be a laugh, but was nothing but devils and dust.

I leaned in. "Seriously, where are all your friends?"

"They not my friends," Alana said, her tone bitter and weary.

I raised a brow. "Colleagues?"

"You could say that. Though I don't know that all of them would."

"Ouch. What happened?"

She opened her mouth to speak, then stopped. She reached for the shot glass instead, sipping at it. Then she said, "They went to some sports bar. To watch the game."

"Why? You've all been drinking here every night since you came to town."

"Yeah, well, it was close to the dive site."

I nodded slowly. If you'd asked me three weeks ago if the FBI had a dive team, I would'nta had a clue. But everyone in these parts knows now. They know because it's part of the biggest story to come along in years. Little baby Leah, all of two, fell from a bridge into the Eno River over a week ago. Authorities have been searching for her ever since. Alana and her cohorts got called in five days ago, diving in the most probable area for Leah to have ended up, based on currents. Evenings, they came into the bar together, not saying much to anyone local. I only knew they were FBI from the news, though Alana confirmed that to me the second time we chatted.

That had been the night we actually shared a couple of drinks at the bar. I think she was glad to get away from her male counterparts and have an easy drink with another woman. We both had to deflect a couple of hopefuls during the time we sat talking, but Yonder is friendly place, and while no means no, I noticed it isn't met with a whole lot of bruised ego.

I wished it was a place I might be able to come back to.

I lifted my glass. "Here's to being a lone wolf while the little puppies run together."

Alana gave me another half-hearted snort, but raised her shot glass and clinked it with mine. She polished off the remainder of the shot, and I waved to Eryk for another round.

"Can I ask you something?"

"What's that?"

"Did you join the FBI and become a diver, or were you already a diver and you joined the FBI?"

"The second one."

"How's that work?"

"How's what work?"

"I mean, do you only just dive for them? Or are you, like, a cop and you dive when they need divers?"

Alana took a slug of her beer. "The second one again. I'm an agent. Diving is an ancillary duty."

"Ants-uh-what?"

She grinned a little. "An additional, secondary duty. I have a caseload, but when the dive team gets called out, I respond."

I nodded that I understood. "You live in Raleigh, then?"

"Yeah."

"You're not working the actual case? The one with the little girl."

"No. I'm just diving."

"It's sad," I said. "What happened to her, I mean."

"Yeah."

"Leah," I said, and the little girl's name hung in the air between us. I saw Alana swallow hard. Then she took another drink of her beer, finishing it.

As if on cue, Eryk arrived. He muttered a few pleasantries, but was quick and efficient and then was gone. Like I said, all good bartenders have a sense of these things.

I raised my glass again. "To Leah," I said softly.

"Leah," Alana whispered, raising hers. This time, she threw back the entire shot.

I took a sip. "I don't mean to pry," I began.

"But you're going to anyway," Alana interrupted me.

I hesitated, then lifted my shoulders in apology. "I'm just wondering if the news is getting everything right or not. Some days I think they make up half the news and fill in the rest with what they don't know."

"They've got the gist of this one."

"Yeah? Good."

Alana reached for her fresh beer. "As close as the media every gets, anyway."

I let that sit for a few seconds. Then I said, "The story is that Leah's mama was carrying groceries back from the store, and so Leah was walking alongside her."

Alana nodded, but I could see she knew something more.

"Here's what I can't figure," I said. "How is that woman not in jail right now? I mean, letting a toddler walk across that rickety old bridge? That ain't right. It's poor mothering. That should be against the law."

"It is. It's called neglect."

"Then why wasn't she charged?"

Alana looked at me closely, as if weighing something. Then she asked, "Where do you work? You never told me."

"At Francine's," I told her truthfully. "It's a breakfast place just off I-85."

"You wait tables?"

"When it gets busy, sure. I manage the place."

Alana looked relieved.

"Why do you ask?"

She smiled grimly. "The way you're asking me questions, I thought you might be a reporter, working me for a story."

I chuckled. "Not me."

"Then why are you interested in this?"

"Everyone's interested, ain't they?" I took a sip. "But if I'm being honest, you just looked like maybe you needed to talk. If you'd rather I leave –"

I started to stand.

"No." Alana held out her hand to stop me. "I'm sorry. That was rude of me." She shook her head. "Being in law enforcement has made me extra suspicious, I guess."

I settled back into my seat. "Now that's interesting."

"What is?"

"You saying, being in law enforcement. Not being a cop."

She actually wrinkled her nose. "I'm not a cop. I'm a federal agent."

"And that ain't a cop because…"

"Because it's federal," she said. "Cops are local. Maybe state. Not federal."

I held up my hands. "Hey, I watch over hash slingers serving truckers and tourists, so you can't expect me to know the difference."

"No, I suppose not. Most people don't."

I took another drink and thought about it for a second. Then I said, "So I'm a little confused, I guess."

"About what?"

"Well, if the FBI is federal, why are you all investigating this thing with baby Leah?"

Alana hesitated, averting her gaze. She lifted her glass to her lips and took a long drink. When she put it back on the table, she turned her gaze to me. I looked back at her, my expression open.

"I don't know if I can say," Alana finally muttered.

"If you can't, you can't," I said, easily enough. I finished my own drink and waved to Eryk. "I just don't know how all that stuff works, that's all."

Alana remained silent until Eryk arrived with a fresh round. He cleared our empty glasses away and strolled easily back to the bar. In the short time I'd been coming here, no matter how fast the man worked, I never saw him seem to be in a hurry.

"Fuck it," Alana muttered. She took a deep breath and looked at me. Then she raised her glass.

I lifted mine, tapping it against hers.

"To truth," Alana said.

I smiled. "I'll drink to that."

We drank.

Alana chased hers with a swallow of beer, finishing off that glass and pushing it away. As she reached for the new one Eryk had just brought, she said, "I'm going to tell you something. It's all going to be in the news by tomorrow, so it doesn't matter."

I rotated my glass in a slow circle, keeping my expression open and interested. "What will be in the news?"

Alana took a deep breath. "All of it. She thought for a second. "Most of it, anyway." She leaned forward, lowering her voice even though the bar was nearly empty. "For starters, the reason we got called in was because the locals suspected a kidnapping."

I looked at her in surprise. "Kidnapping?"

She nodded. "The mother is divorced from the Leah's father. Mark something or other. He only sees the girl once a month. Apparently, there's some kind of custody beef between them, with him claiming she was an unfit mother."

"They think the dad took her?"

"No, not anymore. But for a while, they did. That's why they called us."

"The dad?" I asked. "That wasn't in the news."

"Nope. That's because we debunked it, after we looked into him. Hard. His family, too."

"Family?"

"His folks are gone, but we did backgrounds on his brothers and sisters, and talked to them. It wasn't the dad."

"But you're still investigating?"

"Once we take on a case, we aren't giving it back until it's done."

I shook my head in confusion. "I still don't get how the story went from a little girl falling off a bridge to a kidnapping. It doesn't make any sense."

"She lied."

40

"She? The mother?"

Alana nodded again. "She told all kinds of stories to the locals, and then to us. The one about Leah falling in was just the one that made it out to the public."

"Because that's what you think happened?"

"That isn't what happened." Leah took a drink, watching me while she swallowed.

I frowned. "How do you know this? You said you were just diving, looking for the little girl. Not working the case."

Alana set her bottle back down. "I'm not. But the lead agent is a friend of mine. We used to... we used to be involved." A small shadow seemed to cross her face, then it was gone. "We're still friends. We talk. He likes to bounce things off of me."

"I'll bet."

That struck us both as funny, and we spent a few seconds laughing about it. It was an honest laugh, and it felt good in the middle of all this dark shit.

"So this guy who likes bouncing," I finally said. "He knows what really happened?"

"He thinks so."

"What does he think?"

Alana gave me another appraising look, but it only lasted a second or two. Then she said, "He thinks the mother threw that little girl right over the side of the bridge."

Tears clouded my eyes. Just hearing those words brought such a terrible image to mind that I couldn't help it. I wiped at them, but more came behind. I glanced up at Alana. Her eyes shone, but her cheeks were dry.

"I'm sorry," I mumbled. "It's just so horrible."

"I know." Alana took a drink. "It's horrible that it happened. It's horrible that David knows she did it. And it's horrible that he can't prove it."

I dabbed my eyes with a napkin, not caring if my mascara smeared. "He can't prove it?" I repeated.

"Not in any way that would work in a court of law," Alana said, her tone flat. "All he has is a missing girl and mother telling different stories about it. Any defense attorney worth half a shit can chalk that up to her distress, and good luck getting a jury to think otherwise."

"That's awful."

"That's the game." This time, it was Alana who waved Eryk over for another round. "It's rigged in favor of the criminals. This rule of evidence, that rule of procedure, what is probable cause, and what adds up to beyond a reasonable doubt..."

She trailed off, and we let the silence sit again. Eryk set us up and cleared us off, but I saw him cast a discerning look at us both. My guess was that he'd be suggesting a taxi if we ordered another one anytime soon.

We didn't toast this round, each of us taking a small sip to claim the drink. Then we sat quietly for a bit. I knew I had to wait for her to speak first, and eventually she did.

"He was hoping there would be evidence on the body." Alana spoke softly, almost reverently. "If we found it."

"And you did," I guessed.

She nodded.

That was why the guys on her team went to a loud bar with a game on big TVs. To blow off steam, or to celebrate. And finding that little body is what brought her to this bar, a happier, quieter place on a Tuesday night.

I leaned in. "Was it you?" I asked. "Did you find her?"

She shook her head. "Thank God, no. It was Zack. He found her pinned under a rock..." She stopped, and took a drink before continuing in a shaky voice. "Right where the currents predicted she'd be, if she made it this far."

I had some of my own drink, waiting.

Alana took a deep breath and let it out. "She looked about like you'd expect after being in the water for that long. It runs cold this time of year, so that was a blessing."

"Was she...?"

"Beaten?" Alana shook her head. "No. She had a few obvious post-mortem scrapes from being in the river, but no signs of abuse. None of the evidence David was hoping for."

"There's still a chance, though, isn't there?" I asked. "You'll examine her closely, right?"

"Forensics will, sure. And maybe we'll get lucky and find something that wasn't apparent to the naked eye. Maybe the X-Rays will show old breaks and healed bones, or other signs of abuse." Alana paused. "But I don't think so."

"Why not?"

"That's just what my gut says."

"But Mark said she was an unfit mother. Couldn't that mean abuse?"

"It could," Alana said. "But I don't think so. At least not the physical kind. I think what he meant was the plain old don't-give-a-shit kind of being unfit. And I think he may have been right."

"What makes you think that?"

"David told me things. He thinks that this woman just got sick and tired of having the responsibility of a two-year-old and pitched her over the side of that bridge." She shrugged. "Or maybe she did it for the attention. Munchausen-by-proxy, that sort of thing. Either way, it doesn't matter. He can't prove it, and I don't think the forensics are going to help. So this crazy bitch is going to get off scot free, with all the public sympathy to boot. She'll probably go on the talk show circuit, write a book, all that shit. And the fact that she was ever considered a suspect will just serve as ammunition for her to paint law enforcement in a bad light and make her out to be more of a victim."

"That's fucked up."

Alana raised her glass silently and drained it. She waved to Eryk, then turned to me. "Welcome to my world. There's little justice in it, you want the truth. And there's nothing I can do about it. Things just have to run their course." She smiled, a little drunkenly. "Like that goddamn river did."

Eryk appeared at the table. "How's it going, ladies?"

"It'd go better if you had another round with you," Alana said, her words slurring slightly. I could tell she was at the front end of that wave, and that all the fast drinking we'd been doing still had some more damage to do before that wave crashed.

Eryk smiled cordially. "How about we slow things a bit, and work in an iced tea first?"

"Only if it's a Long Island," Alana said.

"I'm just looking out for you," Eryk said. Then he added, "Officer."

The extra word got through to Alana. She didn't bother to correct him that she was an agent, but the use of the title seemed to serve as some kind of a reminder. She nodded several times. "You're a good man. Think you could call me a cab?"

"You bet." He turned to me, but I shook my head.

"I can call someone."

Eryk nodded and went to the bar.

Alana put her hand over mine. "Thanks for listening," she whispered. "I haven't been able to talk to anyone about this. I can't seem weak around the guys, so... well, thanks."

I squeezed her hand. "Stay strong, sister."

We sat and talked until the cab arrived. Alana gave me a hug before she headed out of the bar and got inside the vehicle.

I stayed at the table, finishing my drink slowly. I thought about everything Alana had told me. The terrible truth of what that mother did, and the terrible image of her doing it. I thought of baby Leah alone in that river, tossed and pulled along until she ended up pressed against that rock down near the river bed.

Justice, Alana said. There was precious little of it. Sometimes, if you let the system run its course, things found their way to that point. Most times, not. She'd been right about that.

I swiped open my cell phone and dialed my cousin's number. He answered on the second ring.

"Mark?"

"Yeah?"

"It's like you thought."

"Fuck."

"Yeah."

"I knew it." After a moment, he asked, "You want me to come get you?"

"No. I'm going to sit a bit longer."

We hung up.

Eryk brought me another, convinced my ride was coming. And it would eventually. All things that need to happen will, eventually.

Including justice.

RAYMOND CHANDLER'S CHAMPAGNE COCKTAIL

Rum
Mango
Mint
Lime
Soda

*"I used to like mine with champagne.
The champagne as cold as Valley Forge
and about a third of a glass of brandy
behind it."*
– Raymond Chandler

Amounts have been left out. Live a little.

GABRIEL VALJAN
POPCORN

"Joe sent me."

The door grille stayed open, and the eyes lingered for the once-over before someone clapped it shut. The verdict was an eternity. He heard the bolt thrown and a chain slide. He was in Yonder, a watering hole known for its cocktails and brew.

"I have to frisk you."

The next stage of acceptance. A jumping-jack without the jump, he spread 'em and counted the number of lightbulbs in the chandelier, while damp hands patted him up and down and all around, as if he were a chicken with the feathers still attached.

Five. Five light bulbs inside a veil of chains.

The only contraband the doorman would find on his person was a small flip-pad, an even smaller bookie's pencil for taking notes, and a wallet. He carried enough money to unstick any charge of vagrancy. He had ID.

Several forms of identification. Those got some love. Their eyes met again; this time he could smell the man's breath. Mint. Probably Pepsodent. A fat thumb peeled through the cards, one for each newspaper in North Carolina.

"A regular tar boiler, aren't you? Profession?"

"Newshawk."

"I can see that. I can read."

Therein lies the potentially lethal mistake of the newshound in the field: assume nothing about literacy. A man can know his letters with his mouth, and not with his eyes. Wallet returned, lettuce intact to buy drinks, and several names to go with the body, the bouncer then grabbed some shirt and tie, turned his head to his boss for the final okay. The nod from the barkeep, a man named Pruitt, could either mean the tie became a noose, or he received a pardon at the last second and could stay.

"He's good."

The large hand released him and pointed to a table against the brick wall. No other words needed, the reporter moved without further encouragement.

Pruitt he had heard of, but never met, and the proprietor headed his way, with a bottle in hand and two short glasses cupped in the other. A complementary drink was a common courtesy, a leftover from the old days of saloons and brothels, when Jill let Jack stay on top of the hill for a price. A barback tended to eclectic customers. A biker in full Harley-Davidson regalia was reading one of Pruitt's books, while next to him a gamecock was trying and failing to score a phone number from the lady next to him.

"Joe sent you, huh," Pruitt said. "How'd you come to know tonight's password?"

"The man who called you on the phone, the guy who set the date and time, he said you agreed to the phrase."

Pruitt's lips twisted, fingers rubbed his chin in thought, or to scratch the itch from shaving. The newsman's sources said Pruitt used to sport a goatee, but his wife Lana had asked him to do away with it; there was bawdy speculation behind the request. There was evidence to support that hearsay. Pruitt was thinner than reported, which could be attributed to either Lana withholding favors until he swept the blade, or her shirking flavor in her cooking. Pruitt looked like the kind of man who enjoyed good food and better living. As for quirks, Pruitt spelled his first name the wrong way, Eryk for Eric, and when he signed books, he crossed out his name and signed above the printed name.

Pruitt, author and business owner, was standing there too long, and the barback was eyeing the table, so the journalist tendered reassurance.

"Joe, as in Joseph Mitchell, is my editor. He sits in a small office in front of a large typewriter, wanting a story that'll sell. The maestro's lost his touch at the keys, so he sent me here."

"To interview Popcorn?"

"Correct."

The brown bottle with the sacred stuff inside was set on the table without any noise. The glasses clinked instead. Pruitt seemed to have bought the subscription.

"That there is a bottle of his finest brew," he said. "One glass is yours, the other is for your guest. No guarantee Popcorn will show, though I did put word out to him. The man is inclined to suspicion, like a bent tree, on account of his history with revenue men."

"I'd heard of his recent troubles. Lawmen couldn't find his still. You can't levy a tax if you can't find the tiger in the woods." The newsman turned over the short glasses and waited for Pruitt to say something because the man remained there, fixed while the barback behind him stared forlorn like a basset hound at an empty rocking chair.

"Now, I'm no scholar, but way I understand it, that if asked, an officer of the court has to declare himself one, if he is one. Are you?"

"Nope, and your man at the door also confirmed I'm not armed."

Pruitt pointed to the uncorked whiskey. "Imbibe while you wait. If he shows, he shows." Pruitt walked away, stopped and returned. "Lana will be out with some fried green tomatoes and boiled peanuts. Oh, and mind your manners if Pop brings Cue Ball with him."

Cue Ball was Popcorn's companion, a mix of Catahoula Leopard and hound of dubious pedigree. As for lineage, Popcorn said his four-legger might have had kin in Louisiana where the Catahoula Hog Dog originated—and his canine did have the telltale cracked-glass eyes—but Popcorn insisted Cue Ball was a plotter, as in Plott Hound, and had more North Carolina tar in him than most of the pine trees in the state.

The paperman poured himself a dram and waited.

Popcorn himself was shrouded in mountain mist. Literally. He seldom volunteered to come down from his mountain in Tennessee. His nickname was born of assault and frustration; hungry after some suds, he fed a bar's popcorn machine a coin and the contraption denied him his handful of kernels, so he 'borrowed' a cue ball from a nearby game and bashed the machine to hell for his prize. Forever hence, he was called Popcorn, though legal records indicate his Christian name was Marvin Sutton.

He surveyed the establishment. Pruitt ran a clean and tight shop. Hardly a dust mote in the air, and nary a peanut shell or pretzel on the hardwood floors. Artwork from local artists hung from the wall. Near the bar, a modest bookcase displayed Pruitt's tomes, along with volumes from other scribes. The cover of a book with a pair of black hands together in prayer faced the columnist.

The bar Yonder had changed hands several times. Unlike other places, Pruitt obtained the best gin, so there was no need to mask juniper berries done wrong with a variety of frou-frou ingredients. The correspondent reviewed the cardstock on his table, which looked like a cadet at The Citadel standing at attention.

The drinks menu offered the standards from the southern repertoire, such as the Alabama Slammer, Chatham Artillery Punch, Mint Julep, Old Fashioned, Ramos Gin Fizz, Sazerac, Seelbach cocktail, and that notorious booze bomb from NOLA's Hotel Monteleone, the Vieux Carré. While whiskey was on offer, Popcorn's bourbon was never blended into cocktails. Pruitt used Jim Beam or Maker's Mark for those calls.

"Here you go," a woman said. Lana, he presumed. She disappeared faster than the two baskets had landed on the table. Boiled peanuts and fried green tomatoes, just as Pruitt had promised.

He sampled. Sliced 3/8ths, the slices of tomato held both bite and spice.

Worried that Popcorn would be a no-show, he passed time by taking in the room. The low idle of conversations and the music said the hatreds of the world stood outside Yonder's door. A sign above the register forbade discussions of politics and religion. Elsewhere, a placard warned customers that martinis were stirred; shaken, it reminded patrons, was a form of domestic violence. Pruitt's place used a Y shaped as a martini glass with a green olive pierced with a toothpick for its logo.

The door opened and every pair of eyes looked up. The ink slinger was used to it, having been inside courtrooms, on various county steps, and within numerous police departments. This time it was different.

Popcorn had arrived.

The dog at the man's side gave the doorman pause as to why he shouldn't lay hands on the legendary moonshiner. Marbled eyes glanced up, assessed the bouncer. One false move and the animal would've had the man's throat in his jaws, and the bruiser knew it. He bypassed the frisk, as if to say Popcorn is southern royalty.

Which he was.

Pruitt moved from behind the bar, like a frog with wings. Popcorn came in wearing what he'd been wearing every day of his life since he left the schoolhouse: bib overalls, a plaid shirt underneath, and a long hillbilly beard. He removed his hat the moment he entered.

Lana had intercepted Popcorn before her husband reached the landing. Lana said nothing about Cue Ball, although an animal on the premises where food and drink were served was technically against the law. Raised with a respect for boundaries and property, Lana asked for permission to touch the dog. Popcorn said some Choctaw word and the dog stepped forward and offered his head. Popcorn asked her if she had raw sardines, since Cue Ball was fond of them. The dog's ears twitched at the sound of the sibilant word sardines. Lana sent her husband into the kitchen for a plate.

"You're the reporter, ain't you?" Popcorn said.

"I am. Please, have a seat, some food and a drink. I appreciate you driving down here to speak with me. Hope the trip didn't inconvenience you any."

"Ain' no Junior Johnson in my three-jugger, but I made good time."

Part of the mythology was that Popcorn had purchased a green Ford Fairmont with three jugs of his hooch. If Robert Johnson, Mississippi Delta bluesman extraordinaire, selling his soul for six-strings was apocryphal, then Wilkes County, North Carolina's native son Robert Glenn 'Junior' Johnson was the real deal. His daddy had made white lightning, and Junior used to run it on dirt roads before he became a NASCAR legend.

"See there, you're having a taste of my likker. Thoughts?"

"Sweet and aromatic."

"You can put away the lace panties, son. My shine was intended to be good enough that you'd love your mother-in-law and not fall down blind doing it. One question for you before I sit, you any good with addition?"

"I'm a writer, not a mathematician."

"And I'm a mountain moonshiner. A still, like words, requires exactitude, precise words in the right order, otherwise it's to Kingdom Come by the fastest means possible."

Popcorn's way of saying he wanted the whole truth and no lipstick or ass-kissing.

"No morning thunder when you read my column, sir. I promise."

"Good."

The chair shuddered against the floorboards. Popcorn sat down, said the interview would be over when he pulled a drink from the bottle on the table. Lana placed two cold glasses of water on the table and disappeared. Popcorn's thank-you hung in the air in her wake.

Other patrons tried not to listen, but did. The couple closest to their table strained the wood in their chairs to catch every word.

Popcorn scooped up a handful of boiled peanuts. He chewed and swallowed, eyes intent on the newspaperman in front of him. A handful later, Lana delivered sardines and a small bowl of water for the guest below.

"Heard you had troubles with lawmen," the journalist said.

"Ever wonder why government is so hot for whiskey?"

"Lost revenue?"

Popcorn leaned back. "Don't you boys carry pen and paper?" The reporter put his hand inside his jacket and came out with the goods. "Good on you, on being prepared," Popcorn said and smiled. "I was about to say that whiskey ain't about lost revenue in the till, nor is it about aidin' and abettin' fornication and corruption of morals. Hell, whiskey ain't even a southern affair. Folks in this country been making whiskey before the nation was born. Know where? I'll tell ya: frontier and Pennsylvania."

"You're talking about the Whiskey Rebellion."

"My people call it the Insurrection, taxation without representation. Any veterans in your line?"

"Back to the Revolutionary War."

"Then you know veterans been fucked bowlegged since time immemorial. George Washington and his brethren elites needed to pay the bills for the War for Independence, and skirmishes with Injuns out west, where folks there had no help or protection from George and Company."

"Hence, the whiskey tax," the newsman answered.

"Forthwith and thenceforth, the common man was fucked, in earnest and in perpetuity."

A customer approached, begged forgiveness for the intrusion. He attempted to invite Popcorn to his home in Maggie Valley to sample his recipe. Unbeknownst to the intruder, Popcorn had been born and bred in Maggie before he moved to his current residence in Parrottsville, Tennessee. Popcorn graciously declined the invite, but not before he asked after the elk in the area. Elk still visited the Valley.

Twenty minutes of conversation later, the baskets of peanuts and tomatoes empty, Popcorn didn't take kindly to the next interloper. Big and brash best described the boyfriend from the next table. He and the girlfriend had been eavesdropping. Not two minutes into his oratory, he reminded every inquiring ear that he had attended Harvard, where he obtained an MBA, which he said qualified him to take Popcorn's business to the next level. Popcorn listened and listened. The man offered a handsome sum to buy Popcorn's recipe.

"Son, I don't know you or your people, but you might as done told me that you played ball from UVA." Popcorn's remark about the south's oldest rivalry elicited a ripple of laughter around the room. "Tell you what, Crimson, I'll give you the recipe for free, if you can land a kiss on Cue Ball's snout."

"Kiss him?"

"Sweet and innocent, like you kiss your momma."

"Free?"

"Free and clear as sky on a bright summer day." Popcorn pointed to the newspaperman. "I'll script the recipe on paper from this gentleman. You can have it notarized, and a Harvard man, like you, is bright enough with figures that you can scale the ingredients accordingly; in fact, if your mistress here can land a kiss on Cue Ball, I'll drive you both to Tennessee myself, provide you with room and board, and show you how to make a batch. What do you say?"

The man, offended, lifted his chin up. "And what makes you think she's my mistress?"

"Put out your left hand."

He hesitated. The 'girlfriend' stepped forward. She reached for his hand and her dirtied beau pulled it away. "You're nothing more than an oversized meadow muffin, you lying sack of shit," she said.

"Take your hands off me," he said.

She looked to Popcorn for an explanation after she failed to obtain proof.

Popcorn said to her, "Tan line on his wedding finger says he removed his wedding band." Popcorn then turned to Harvard. "Two eyes and lived experience are worth more than whatever it says on your diplomas. Now, how about it? Show some love to Cue Ball."

The dog sat up and leaned back on his haunches and looked up at the businessman. Cue Ball's tongue flopped out, and without panting, he blinked.

"Never mind," the man answered. He realized within two steps his paramour had not followed him. "Are you coming or not?"

"I'm staying."

"And how will you get home?"

"I'll manage."

Popcorn turned in his chair. "My friend here will drive her home and, by that, I mean he'll use his car, I think."

The man stormed off. "Bless his heart," Popcorn said and rose, surrendering his chair to the lady. She sat down, and he poured her a drink into the unused glass.

Lana appeared tableside, handing Popcorn a small bag. "For the road," she said, and explained that the bag contained popcorn dusted with a blend of chili powder, cinnamon, and sugar. He thanked her, he thanked the reporter.

"Hold on, Popcorn," the newsman said. "You didn't answer the last question before we were interrupted. You were saying you had your epitaph ready for your gravestone. You didn't tell me what it says."

"Indeed, I had not. If the lady here will pardon my French, I'll tell you."

"Please do," she said.

Popcorn put his hat on, and told Cue Ball he was ready to leave. "The marker is in keeping with my disposition towards authority and injustice. Engraved on my stone is, Popcorn Said Fuck You."

And with that, Popcorn walked off, Cue Ball in tow, and before he vacated the premises, he raised his hat to the owner, "Got to put a lid on the mason jar. May your flame burn blue and the world not make you blind, Mr. Pruitt."

JEFFERY DEAVER'S CARTE BLANCHE

Crown Royal
Cointreau
Angostura

"Shaken, not stirred."

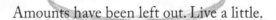

Amounts have been left out. Live a little.

WILL VIHARO
LIVING PROOF
(A VIC VALENTINE VIGNETTE)

A s we grow older and closer to our unknown individual expiration date, every extra day of life feels like a stay of execution. But everyone's death sentence is passed the day we're born, uniformly upheld without any exact dates for us to plan around, and we can only evade the inevitable for so long. I'd been hired to find out why some guy had died clear across the country. But the thing is, the reason we all die ultimately doesn't matter, because sooner or later, it finds us, whoever and wherever we are. Some sooner than others, of course. Whether luck of the draw or fate, it's totally irrelevant. I wasn't ready to go yet, but then as I said, Death doesn't share its appointment calendar with anyone in advance.

North Carolina, my unlikely destination in this particular case, was never a state I thought I'd wind up in. State of depression, state of confusion, state of decay, sure. But North Carolina just never made my travel radar, any more than South Carolina or North Dakota or South Dakota for that matter. They just seemed like places cut in two that could've just as easily remained as one, but then you could say that about a lot of things, like sandwiches or marriages. Then again, maybe not.

The place where I was told I could get some information was a cozy little joint called the Yonder Southern Cocktails and Brew. I was instructed by my mysterious client to ask for the owner, whose name was Eryk, spelled with a 'y' for some reason. Apparently that aberration didn't affect the pronunciation, so it didn't matter. Not to me, anyway.

"I'm looking for Eryk with a 'y'," I said to the guy behind the bar as I took a seat. He was a clean cut dude with an organically friendly manner, which made me immediately suspicious, but then I was raised in Brooklyn.

He smiled quizzically. "Eryk. With a 'y'."

"Yeah."

"You mean, like, with a question?"

"Several."

"I have one first. Why do you want to see him?"

"For some answers."

"What makes you think he has them?"

"I don't. Only way to find out is to ask."

"Well, you found him."

"You're Eryk? With a 'y'?"

"Yeah. Who are you?"

"Vic Valentine. I'm a dick from San Francisco."

"I hear there's loads of 'em out there."

"Well, I'm the biggest." That didn't come out right or maybe it did. I'm not at adept at self-assessment anymore than I am at self-censorship.

"You must be good," he said.

"Why?"

"Exactly."

"I mean, good at what?"

"You're a detective and you already found who you're looking for."

"Well, I was told to ask for you here, so I kinda had a head start."

"Who told you to ask for me?"

"I can't tell you that." The reason being I didn't really know.

"Well, then I can't tell you anything, either. Guy like you walks in out of the blue, what am I supposed to do? You could be a hit man for all I know."

"I look like a hit man to you?"

"A short one."

"Short? What, like Joe Pesci?"

He laughed. "I'm just giving you a hard time. What's with the suit and tie? Aren't you hot?"

I loosened my skinny tie a bit. My shiny sharkskin suit did stand out amid all the T-shirts and shorts and sandals surrounding me, but then I was a walking anachronism wherever I went. I looked back at the few patrons, sitting around the tables talking about politics like sports, subjects I always avoided. A couple of them gave me the once-over, but not in a menacing or patronizing way. Just passively curious. I avoided eye contact, as I always do. I don't like people and the feeling is generally mutual. "Yeah, well, I have to keep up appearances," I finally said in response.

"Is this snazzy old outfit, like, your uniform?"

"Kinda."

"I always wondered how Jack Lord did it."

"Did what?"

"Wore a suit all the time. In Hawaii."

He won me over with that reference. "Yeah, me too. Speaking of which, any good tiki bars around here?"

"Is that the question you wanted to ask me?"

"No."

"Well, good, because there ain't. Not that I know of. I can make you a Mai Tai if you want."

"The original one with lime juice and orgeat or the touristy one with grenadine and pineapple juice?"

He gave me a funny look, which meant I just ordered a Manhattan.

"Okay, I can make you that. We got premium bourbon. Any particular preference?"

"Bartender's choice."

He just nodded and said, "But unless you tell me why you're here, I'm not answering any questions."

"I'm actually looking for a dead guy."

"I can't make you a Zombie either."

"No, I meant, not his corpse. Just wondering what happened to him, or rather how it happened. I'm told you knew him."

Eryk seemed to ponder the question as he took out his cellphone from a back pocket. At first I was worried he was Googling "How to Make a Manhattan," which was as Basic 101 as the bottle of Wild Turkey he had pulled down from the shelf behind him. Turned out he was just sending a text, or so it seemed. Then he quietly poured the hard booze into a shaker, added the proper amount of sweet vermouth with some bitters, shook it up, and served it to me, up and perfectly chilled. He'd even garnished it with the right type of cherry, too. I took a sip, letting him think it over.

"Without you even telling me, I know who you mean," he said finally.

"Okay. So?"

"So some people are coming over who can help you out."

"Wow. Well, thanks."

"Don't mention it." Suddenly his demeanor was as chilly as my cocktail, but I didn't care. He went about his business, and I just stared at the backlit bar, idly dreaming about Bettie Page because that's what I always do when I'm bored. And even when I'm not.

An indeterminate amount of time passed before two people sidled up on either side of me, taking their seats with a sense of secret purpose. I knew they were there to see me. Eryk came over to greet them.

"Marietta," he said to the attractive woman on my left.

"Eryk," she said.

"Shawn," he said to the big badass on my right.

"Eryk," he said with a nod.

"Sean?" I said. "As in Sean Connery?"

"More like Idris Elba," the big guy said.

"Hey, I got nothing against a black Bond." I was already making a fool of myself. Why waste time, I figured. It was going to happen eventually. Like Death.

"I spell my name differently," he said without missing a beat.

"Than Idris Elba? I can't even spell his."

He shook his head slowly, waiting for me to catch up.

"Oh. Sean. How else can you spell it?"

"Think about it."

I did as I was told. Then it hit me. "Oh! Like Shaun of the Dead."

"Nope."

I thought about it some more. Then I said, "Oh, like Prawn?"

He turned his head and looked me dead in the eyes. Suddenly I had to pee. "I look like a damn prawn to you?"

I shook my head, and then he laughed and slapped me on the back, making me spit out some of my drink. I tried to laugh too, but only drooled. I was embarrassing myself at a record clip, even for me.

I turned to the woman, hoping for a smooth transition back to Coolville. No dice. She was staring at the boozy saliva dripping from my lips. She handed me a napkin. I wiped my mouth and said, "Marietta, yes?"

"Sometimes," she said.

"Not your real name?"

"Why would I tell you if it wasn't? Wouldn't that ruin the whole idea of having an alias?"

"Good point,"

"These folks know the guy you're looking for," Eryk said, coming to my rescue, probably to expedite the conversation so we could all just move on with our lives already. At least that was my motivation.

Feeling intimidated, I said, "Well, I was only told to ask for you."

"You did. And then I asked for my friends here."

That's when both Marietta and Shawn took out their guns and put them on the bar in front of them. Two .45 Colts. Eryk didn't even flinch.

"I didn't know this was an open carry state," I said nervously.

"It's not," Shawn said. "They were concealed first."

"Oh. You a cop?"

"No. I work in a mortuary."

"So you are like Shaun of the Dead."

"Ha ha ha," he said without a trace of amusement. "Haven't heard that one before."

"Guy you're talking about?" Marietta chimed in. "Last time we saw him, he wasn't dead."

"So maybe he died since then," I said.

"I would've noticed," Shawn said. "He's not a customer of mine. Not yet."

"Maybe we're not talking about the same guy," I said.

"Yes, you are," Eryk said.

"How do you know?"

"Because I'm the guy who hired you."

I'd only had one drink, and not even all of it yet, so I couldn't blame my confusion on alcohol, my usual alibi. "You hired me to come out here and find you?"

"Not find me. Ask for me."

"How can this be?"

"Think about it. All you got was a phone call and a wire transfer into your account. You never met me. Until now."

"Why all the subterfuge? And why not just hire someone local?"

"Because we don't want anyone knowing about this. No one around here."

"How did you pick me?"

"Phone book."

"But why me?"

"You're cheap. All I could afford. Plus you agreed to fly out here on your own dime."

"I was figuring you'd reimburse me."

"I'm not. That was included in the fee."

"Aw, shit." I downed the rest of my drink, got up from the stool, and was ready to walk out when Shawn stood up and blocked me, overshadowing me like a total eclipse. I sat back down.

"I don't get it," I said. "But then I don't really get anything."

"You're forgetting something else," Eryk said.

"I've always had a bad memory, at least as I recall."

"I thought you were a detective," Shawn said. "Eye for detail, all that."

"Not really. The only reason I can even remember to jerk off every day is muscle memory."

"TMI," Marietta said.

"Sorry, sometimes I forget myself in the company of ladies."

"You always this crude?" she asked.

"When I was young and stupid."

"What are you now?"

"A lot less young, a little less stupid."

"But still crude."

"I try to be polite. It's not a hard and fast rule."

"I got your hard and fast rule right here," Shawn said. "More like a hard and fast ruler. All twelve inches."

"Hey, a lady is present," I said.

Both Shawn and Marietta laughed again. Eryk didn't. He just kept staring at me, waiting for me to figure out why I was here.

"I'm getting the idea you flew me out here just to mess with me," I said. "Hey, you paid me. Knock yourselves out."

"We want you to kill him," Eryk said flatly.

I was carrying a .38. I hadn't pulled it yet because, for one thing, I was outgunned. They obviously anticipated the fact I was strapped, given my so-called profession. But I wasn't a contract killer by any stretch.

"I thought I was too short to be a hit man," I said.

"Tall enough," Shawn said. "Just aim up."

"What makes you think I would kill someone?"

"Because if you don't, we'll kill you," Marietta said.

"And nobody will miss you," Shawn said. "Even if they did, like your friend Doc out there, they wouldn't be able to find you. See, we

69

offer cremation services at my place of business."

"So it would be like the end of 'Ocean's Eleven'," I said, trying to inject some levity into the suddenly serious proceedings with a random retro-reference.

"What are you talking about?" Marietta asked.

"He means the original," Eryk said. "The old one. With the Rat Pack."

"I never even heard of it," Marietta said.

"Because it sucks," Shawn said.

"Well, you're just going to have to kill me," I said. "I don't even like eating meat. In fact, I'm thinking of becoming a vegan."

"So you don't dig barbecue," Shawn said.

"No, which is why this whole cremating scenario doesn't work for me, either. When I get my ashes hauled, I'm thinking of something else entirely."

"You think we won't kill you?" Eryk said.

"No. For one thing, you have too many witnesses." I gestured behind me to the patrons at the tables, who suddenly had their guns out, too, aimed right at me. It was all a set-up. I felt like I was trapped in a remake of Two Thousand Maniacs (1964), except that had already been remade in 2005 as 2001 Maniacs. Not bad, actually. Still, I didn't want to star in the documentary version.

"What was it I forgot again?" I said.

"When we talked on the phone," Eryk said. "I told you not to book a return flight."

"I thought that was because you'd book it for me."

"He's not," Shawn and Marietta both said in unison. Everyone in the damn bar kept their guns trained on me. I looked yearningly at the door. That's when one of the patrons got up and locked it.

So this was it. I was either going to kill someone or get killed myself. Shawn had mentioned my friend Doc back San Francisco, the only person who really gave a damn about me. They'd done their research. But good. They were right. I didn't really have any friends or family to speak of. No lovers, none that would notice I was suddenly gone, anyway. Maybe my friend Monica. She was a waitress back at Doc's joint, The Drive-Inn. But she'd get over me. I hadn't told her or Doc where I was going, because that was part of the initial instructions. Now I knew why. Eventually the cops would find out I'd bought a one-way ticket to North Carolina. But then the trail would go cold. My dusty remains would get flushed down the toilet and that would be that.

"Okay, just do it," I said. "I don't care."

They all looked at me. "What do you mean, you don't care?" Eryk said.

"Kill me. I got nothing to live for. But do it quick. Find some other sucker."

"I'll just beat you till you agree," Shawn said.

"Go ahead. I'm a glutton for punishment. Ask any of my ex-girl-friends."

"We did," Marietta said. "Including Monica."

"Shit. Did you threaten her?"

"No man," Shawn said. "I called the Drive-Inn and asked for you. She answered. I just told her I was a potential client, asked a few questions, got a few answers, and hung up. She had no idea why. But we know who she is, where she lives. Doc, too. Now you ready to cooperate or not? Because here's the thing: either way, you're gonna burn."

"That sucks," I said. "I hate the heat. That's why I'm thinking of moving to Seattle."

"Ain't gonna happen," Shawn said.

I really hated heat more than anything, so that settled it. Fuck the other guy. "Okay, who do you want me to ice, and why?" I said with resignation.

They all looked at each other, then back at me, and broke into laughter.

"Me," Eryk said. "I want you to kill me."

Then everyone stopped laughing, while I was just getting started. But he was dead serious, or so it seemed.

"This just keeps getting weirder," I said. "But then life is like that. Mine, anyway."

"Just kidding!" Eryk said. Everyone laughed again. "See, we're not criminals. Just crime writers. We're working on an anthology of stories, and we were stuck on a unifying theme. So we pooled our money, searched the Internet, found a sucker, and flew him—meaning you—out here, set up this situation, and took bets on what you'd do, how you'd react to the ultimatum. On top of being a creative project, it was an experiment in human nature."

"And I'm the guinea pig."

"We'll make it up to you, promise!"

"Like how."

"You like to drink, right?"

"You've done your homework."

Shawn then pointed his gun right in my face and said, "First shot on me." Then he pulled the trigger and blasted me right in the face. It was a water pistol, loaded with whiskey.

Then they all started laughing. Again. At my expense. Literally. I still had to buy my own return ticket to San Francisco. Meantime, I was allowed to drink and eat the equivalent, on the house. Marietta offered me a room to stay for a few days.

After that, everyone there bought me drinks. Many drinks. And food. For a week. It turned out to be a nice vacation in a place I never planned to be, but it turned out okay. All I'll say is those Southern belles know how to ring-a-ding-ding. They were all grateful for my unwitting participation.

As Eryk further explained to me after the big reveal, "Now each of us is going to write the same story, meaning this one, but with a different twist ending. We're reading it at our next gathering, called Noir at the Bar. Fortunately for you, this one happens to be your ending."

"This time, anyway," I said. "Cheers."

IAN FLEMING'S VESPER

Gin
Vodka
Lillet Blanc

"Three measures of Gordon's, one of vodka, half a measure of Kina Lillet. Shake it very well until it's ice-cold, then add a large, thin slice of lemon peel. Got it?"
– Ian Fleming (Casino Royale)

Amounts have been left out. Live a little.

TERRI LYNN COOP
OFF-LABEL

As soon as the glass door closed behind me, I stepped aside to get my bearings in the dark bar. I don't like being backlit in a strange place. In the two years since the FBI had shut down the family law firm, I'd learned to take nothing at face value.

"Jewel, over here."

I turned to the sound and smiled, anchored again. Max Gano was exactly where I'd expect to find him, at a corner table with his back to the wall. As I passed the bartender, he said, "Hey, what can I get you?"

"Draft. I used to run a bar. Surprise me with something good."

Max's hugs always felt right. It was good to have someone to trust. Still, my innate caution kept me quiet until I had the frosted mug in front of me and the bartender had withdrawn to the far end to polish glasses. I liked this place already. He understood that we didn't want to be overheard or bothered.

We clicked mugs, and I took a sip. The piquant golden brew had a touch of fruitiness. Summer Ale. My favorite. I drank deep before speaking.

"Okay Max, yesterday I was reading guidebooks about Mount

Rushmore and planning a trip through the Badlands. Why am I in fucking North Carolina?"

"Let's wait for our third. I only want to brief this once. Where's the pooch?"

"Since you told me this is a weekend turnaround, I checked Simon into a doggie spa that cost more than my plane ticket. This had better be worth it. Not that I mind seeing you and Ethan."

As if on cue, the throaty growl of a Harley penetrated the afternoon. He glided to a stop at the windowed bar front before accelerating out of sight. I knew he was checking access and egress. Extreme caution had kept him alive more than once as an undercover operative.

I raised my hand to signal for another round just as the front door opened. Special Agent Ethan Price didn't stay in silhouette any longer than I had. He was in full biker regalia with boots, black jeans, one of his stretched thin t-shirts, and leather vest. The bandana tied into a do-rag softened the lines of the high-and-tight haircut his current office assignment required and he needed a shave. It wasn't just his clothes. He'd adjusted his entire stance and presence to convey that fucking with him was a very bad idea.

I wasn't buying any of it. I threw my arms around his neck and kissed him, molding my body into his. Tension melted out of him as he lifted me off the ground in a monster embrace. When he sat down his normal glower held a hint of a smile.

"What'll it be?" The bartender already had a tray out.

"Whatever's in the keg. I'm not picky. And a refill for my friends."

"Coming right up. Hey, where you from in Texas?"

Ethan's eyes narrowed. With his degree in linguistics, he prided himself on keeping his childhood accent in check.

"Why do you ask?" he said, the words dripping venom.

"Cool your jets, Hoss, I'm just making conversation. You're real good but you can't fool my ear."

"South of Dallas," I said, putting a hand on Ethan's arm.

"You may be but I put him a whole lot farther west. No mind. Just curious. Welcome to Yonder. I'm Eryk, and I own this place." After a quick wipe of the table and fresh coasters, he put down our mugs and disappeared.

Ethan took a drink and grimaced. Evidently, he was pickier than he thought.

"All right Max, out with it. I just spent seven hours in the saddle from Macon. You're lucky, the lead defense attorney has the flu and opening arguments are delayed for a week. The outside world thinks I'm fishing at a buddy's cabin."

Max folded a napkin into a swan and floated it in Ethan's now-untouched beer. "You think I don't know that? It's why I called. I need your help with something. Something off-label."

That got my attention. Max was an FBI fixer. He handled undercover agents and got information where it needed to be. Methods were less important than results. But this one was apparently freelance.

Ethan leaned back and folded his arms across his chest. "I'm listening."

A friend of mine needs her daughter and grandchildren extracted from an unpleasant situation.

I nodded and asked, "Meth or crack?"

"I'm sure it's whatever they can get their hands on in between cooks. She has a rehab set up for the girl and the papers ready to get her custody of the grandbabies."

I had to get my lawyer on. "That's kidnapping."

"I prefer to think of it as an intervention. Seriously, I scoped it out yesterday. The situation is bad. You can smell the ammonia from the main road. It's no place for children. Plus, I owe her big time. She's a friend."

I couldn't resist. "Is she a friend or a friend-friend?"

"The regular kind. Her late husband did me a solid, and I never got to pay it back."

"I understand. What about, you know, DHHS and foster care?"

"The client is, shall we say, impatient. She even insisted I take five grand for expenses. Since none of us need the cash, I figure we can find something worthwhile to do with it."

"Ethan?"

"What the hell, I'm in. I trust Max and owe him a few myself. What's the plan?"

Max smiled, and I groaned inwardly. It looked like I was along for the ride.

"We'll go over the fine details later. The dude is in jail. She and the kids are at their trailer. I thought some theater to convince her we're her old man's contacts will get us in the door. After that, we'll either appeal to her humanity, or take a more direct approach. I figured some shock and awe if we need it, with Jewel as back-up and helping with the rug rats."

"Kids? Me? Have we met?"

Max shrugged and sat back as the bartender came to the table. Ethan handed him the mug with the paper swan in the bottom and said, "Let's try this again. Whatever's in the keg that's not day-after frat party dregs."

A smile told us that the joke hit home.

When he returned with fresh drinks, Ethan dropped the biker from his voice. "You said you're the owner, right?"

"That would be me. Why do you ask?"

"Then you'd know if anything is in the wind."

"Not sure what you're talking about."

"Something's off in the street vibe. Tension. There's a guy that's walked by the front door three times since I got here. Is there anything that has the local factions squaring off? Something keeps pinging my radar."

I put down my mug. I'd been on the business end of this radar many times. It rarely went well. And he was rarely wrong.

"Well, Duke and the Tar Heels are playing tomorrow. Plenty of conflicted loyalties around town and the partying will be hard. I'm expecting a full house."

Ethan raised an eyebrow. "Party favors?"

"Oh yeah. I run a clean place but you can only do so much."

"Anybody giving you any problems?"

"I had to boot some locals night before last. They were disrespecting the ladies. I don't tolerate that. Mostly they were just drunk and stupid. In fact, they took the guts out of that first keg."

"That'd make me surly too."

"You did ask for it."

"True that. Hey, does this place have a back door?"

"Yeah. Past the men's room. It goes to the alley."

Max leaned in. "What're you chewing on, Price?"

"I want to have another look at our guest out there and see if I can draw a bead on whatever's going on. It's cool. I'll be right back." He touched my shoulder and headed toward the back of the room.

Max gulped the last of his beer and pushed his chair back. "If you're cooking something up, I'd better hit the head and maybe check out that alley."

"I thought only girls peed together."

He tossed me a wink and a blown kiss in response.

I'm not sure why but I felt weird sitting at the table by myself. I bundled up our empty glasses, carried them to the bar, and plunked myself on a stool.

"You trying to cut into my tip?"

I laughed. "No, just force of habit. Empty mugs aren't generating cash."

The smile I got in return was genuine and full of devilment. "In that case, a refill?"

"Make it iced tea. I need to pace myself."

He waggled his eyebrows. "Not on my account."

As he stepped into the back for my tea, the door darkened, lightened, and darkened again. I caught movement in my peripheral vision and another habit kicked in. My hand strayed to the Sig Sauer P229 Nitron in my waistband holster.

"Sweetheart, don't even think about it. In fact, stand up and let me see your hands." The low voice jangled with tension.

It took everything I had to not look toward the back door. I didn't want to tip them to Ethan or Max. Instead, I focused on the two intruders. Average height and build but I wasn't interested in the police report. One held a piece-of-shit pistol, and the other cradled a sawed-off shotgun. That was more than enough firepower to repaint the interior of this place.

"I'm sorry. Please don't shoot." I put a high whine and burble of fear into my voice.

At that moment, the owner came out with a pitcher of tea.

"Why thank you, Mr. Yon-der, but I'd rather have a beer," said the guy with the shotgun.

I had to admire Eryk's cool. He put the tea on the bar, flicked his wrist toward the well, and came up with two bottles dripping crushed ice. With a practiced move, he flipped an opener, and both caps went flying.

"Now empty the register."

"Ain't got shit here, Bro. I've barely been open for two hours."

"Bullshit. Last night I heard you talking to your wife about needing a double till because of the football crowd. Now hand it over."

"That means I've got an extra fifty in singles. I'm serious. You're welcome to it but it ain't nothing." The register rang, and he placed the stack of bills on the bar.

While this was going on, the pistol dude kept his eyes on me. I wasn't sure if it was good news or bad. Since I'd expected a weekend of after-hours fun with Ethan, underneath my unbuttoned shirt I was wearing a skimpy tank top with a bra that put everything front and center. A vine of small tattooed flowers adorned the still garish scar that cut diagonally from my shoulder across my breasts.

"Hey, let's see what she's got," he said, gesturing with the pistol.

"Oh, she's got plenty but we don't have time." Shotgun pocketed the cash.

"Just a second. I want a souvenir." Pistol dude grabbed my gold locket and broke the chain. Tears threatened. That was a gift from my late Uncle Jimmy. I didn't flinch when he trailed his knuckle down my neck toward my cleavage. I'd been through fire. This was nothing.

"FBI."

The sound was in stereo from in front and behind me filling the narrow space. Ethan advanced with his Mossberg 500 bullpup leveled and alternated between the two robbers. He's not a tall man, but he knows how to dominate a room. They hesitated but not long enough. In the gloom, the leader's finger slipped inside the trigger guard of the sawed-off.

The click of my P229 leaving the Blade-Tech holster was loud in the tension. I didn't care.

"GUN," I yelled as I sighted and squeezed the trigger. A neat hole appeared in the leader's forehead as my would-be attacker stumbled backward fumbling his pistol. Ethan took the opportunity and pumped a round of buckshot into his chest and belly. After safeing his weapon, he recovered my locket from the dying man's still twitching hand.

In the minute it'd taken this to go down, the bartender had ducked out of sight, the two dripping bottles still on the bar.

Max came from the back hallway and holstered his weapon. It wasn't his service piece. We really were off the radar with this one.

"Let me think," was all he had to say.

After a few seconds, he said, "Jewel, hand it over."

I knew where he was headed. I wiped the grip and said, "Dammit, I just got this."

He covered his hand with his shirt before taking it. "Don't worry, Sweetheart, I know where they keep more. What about the bullets?" He swapped my pistol for the one that had flown out of the dead man's hand.

"I polished them before loading. Remember, I used to represent criminals in court."

"Good girl."

Ethan wiped down the shotgun.. Then he sat at the bar, picked up a beer, and drank half before speaking.

"Okay Eryk, you can come out now. Odds are someone has called the cops. We really don't want to be mixed up in this. Is there any chance you'd be willing to take the credit? To me it looks like they had a fight, one shot the other, and then you took care of business second-amendment-style. You good with that?" He stressed the last four words in such a way that suggested being good with it was the prudent choice.

The bartender stood and said, "Texas, I'm good with it. One question though."

"If I can."

"Y'all really FBI?"

Ethan laid the Mossberg on the bar and shrugged.

Our host nodded in understanding as a faint wail of sirens became audible.

Max threw a rubber-banded bundle of cash on the bar and said, "That ought to cover our tab and any ancillary expenses. Come on, you two, the alley awaits."

The sirens cut abruptly as we exited onto the street a block down. Cops bailed through the front door of the bar. We all gawked and gave the scene the once-over like good civilian lookie-loos. Ignoring it would be suspicious. Act like a local and people will forget in half an hour. Act out of character and they'll never forget.

Max gave us an address to meet later to work on the plan to extract our targets. Before we split up to head to our vehicles, I asked, "That cash you threw on the bar was the five grand you got for this off-label favor, wasn't it?"

"I figure he earned it. Now, get gone and be careful."

I dropped the gold locket in my shirt pocket and said, "It's what we do."

HABAÑERO
MARGARITA

Tequila
Habanero
Lime
Lemon

"She was the third beer. Not the first one, which the throat receives with almost tearful gratitude, nor the second, that confirms and extends the pleasure of the first. But the third, the one you drink because it's there, because it can't hurt, and because what difference does it make?"
– Toni Morrison

Amounts have been left out. Live a little.

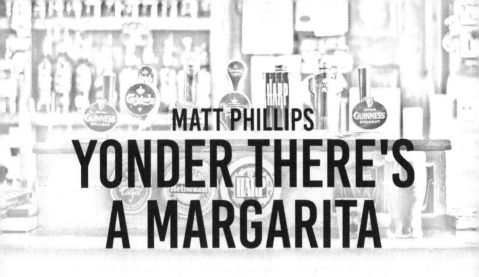

MATT PHILLIPS
YONDER THERE'S A MARGARITA

F reddie the Cripple liked himself a decent margarita.

None of that pre-made shit from the grocery store. He liked himself a margarita like they did it down in Veracruz, where he used to pick up Mary Jane and fly it into San Diego for a drug cartel. Freddie the cripple lost that job and got his nickname at the same time—he ditched a glider plane full of ganja off the coast of Tijuana. Saw the US Coast Guard chopper just across the border and thought: Fuck it. He had a hell of a swim back to Tijuana Beach, but he made it and—after self-medicating at the Safari Club—crossed back to the states a day later. A strip mall doctor in National City tried to reset Freddie's right lower leg, but it was too badly broken.

Hence the limp.

And hence the name: Freddie the Cripple.

He kind of liked the handle and started to introduce himself that way. Like, "How you doing, boss? I'm Freddie the Cripple. At your service." He always added 'at your service.' Figured that got him a lot of business, especially in some of the rougher cities out west. But he also got calls from the east coast. Bash-up jobs for the most part.

That's what this North Carolina thing was—a bash-up job.

◊

But it was a different kind of bash-up job.

He was getting paid to light a guy's office on fire. Some writer, a two-bit writer from what Freddie could tell. Of course, what the fuck did he know—he read Spiderman comics and nudie mags. Never put his eyes to a book this side of paradise. No time. Freddie liked himself some strip clubs and margaritas—why waste precious hours on the written word? What surprised Freddie though, was how the writer had himself a job.

Like, a job-job.

He tended bar at a place called Yonder. It must be the south, Freddie thought, with a name like that. Freddie's contact gave him the name of the bar, said he could start following the writer there. And sure enough, he walked into the joint and who is it but the writer asking him what's his pleasure? Freddie shrugged, hobbled over to the bar, and took his seat. The writer made him a margarita—put his own spicy spin on the thing—and Freddie had been a regular for the five days since. He liked the margaritas. And he liked the writer.

But Freddie the Cripple still had a job to do.

◊

They got to talking one night, Freddie three 'ritas deep and thinking about tequila shots.

Freddie said, "You're a writer, right?"

The writer bent over the bar, thumbed through images on his cell phone. Passed it to Freddie for a look. Some old lady on a beach reading the guy's book. Another one of teenagers reading it in class.

A few images of bums reading it at bus stops and while they begged for cash.

Freddie shrugged and said, "How much you pay the bums to do that, man?"

"Shit, Freddie." The writer shook his head, slipped his phone back in a pocket. "These are my fans, Freddie—my readers. You know what I mean?"

"Shit—I been in here a week straight. The only thing I seen you write is a dirty note on a napkin and give it to that manager."

"She's my wife—I own this place."

"Wait one fucking southern minute—you own this joint?" That, too, surprised Freddie. What kind of fucking writer was this guy? "How you supposed to own a restaurant, write novels, and still have time for going out on the town?"

The writer shrugged, moved down the bar to make drinks for some old geezers. "I'm an enigma, Freddie. What else can I say?"

Freddie the cripple shook his head, finished his margarita. He decided to call his handler, maybe take one more shot at getting clarity about this thing.

◊

The other writer breathed hard over the phone line and said, "What the fuck do you mean, you like the guy?"

Freddie was laying on his bed in Motel 6, watching a spider cross the ceiling while he enjoyed his margarita buzz. "I mean, I like him. And, shit, he's not a writer-writer, is he?"

"The fuck does that mean?"

"I mean, the fucker has a day job. Well, a night job. But it's all the same—he must not make much on the writing thing."

"Let me ask you something: If a guy hears something about another guy, that maybe this one guy is willing to scare the fuck out of somebody for enough money, and then he calls the guy and pays him half the money, don't you think this one guy should do the fucking job and scare the—"

"We're talking four Gs," Freddie said. "It ain't like it's a million bones, is it?"

"That equals my royalty check for the past five years you arrogant fuck of a hood." The other writer was probably spitting on the phone receiver.

"Fine," Freddie the cripple said. "I'll burn down the office, but I want you to tell me why. I mean, shit, if you don't like the guy —why not pay me to kill him?"

The other writer breathed harder into the phone and said, "You'd do that? How much money you want to do that?"

"Christ," Freddie said, "You writers are sick."

◊

Next day, Freddie was sitting outside the writer's house in a rented Dodge Neon. He was listening to a classic rock station—Kansas, Boston, and plenty of Skynyrd—when the writer wandered outside in a vomit-colored bathrobe. He bent to pick up the local paper, raised his eyebrows at the headlines, and then ambled back inside the house. The way it was told to Freddie, the writer had himself an office in the backyard—one of those prefab sheds you get at Home Depot? He cut some windows into it, added a door with glass panels. And inside the office was where the writer kept all his manuscripts. Freddie the cripple guessed that was the point. If he burned the office down, the manuscripts end up ash in a woodpile. It felt a bit unethical to Freddie, like maybe this writer-guy was just trying to do his thing. Make a life for himself. Go on and get his dream. And here Freddie was, a foreigner to this low southern country, about to burn the guy's work down to hell. Well, shit. No matter how Freddie felt about the job, he needed to go through with it. Otherwise, every small town hood from Eureka to the Okenfenokee Swamp was going to hear how Freddie the Cripple didn't get a job done. If that happened, the work would dry up for Freddie. Whether he added 'at your service' to his introductions or not. Forty-five minutes later, as Stevie Ray Vaughn was doubling his trouble on the Neon's car radio, the writer walked out of his house in blue jeans and a t-shirt, got in a beat-to-shit Hyundai, and drove off in a cloud of blue coolant haze. Freddie made a mental note—I run into the writer at the bar tonight, I should let him know how to hunt down a coolant leak. But right now, I got a job to do.

◊

The red gas can dangled from Freddie the cripple's right hand as he lurched around the side of the house. He got to the backyard and spotted the office right away—kind of cute the way the writer put it together. It was small and gray and quaint, like a hobbit house or something. In the glass-paned door, he had those blinds like a detective does in an old movie. And the writing on the door as well. Gold lettering. Freddie couldn't see what the words said, but it didn't matter to him. He was busy picking peppers off a nearby garden plant, popping them into his mouth and chewing like a kid on Halloween. "Shit," Freddie said, "that tastes like good strip club twat." The garden and backyard smelled like chopped vegetables and basil. Either the writer or his wife had a green thumb. Hell, two green

93

thumbs. Looking at the growing vegetables, it made sense to him how the writer owned and ran a restaurant with his wife. And why not? People have all sorts of talents and hobbies. Freddie wandered from plant to plant, picked off tomatoes and radishes and more peppers. He popped them into his mouth one by one.

He licked his lips after chewing everything.

Even felt bad for about half a second.

But then he thought: Shit, nothing a rabbit wouldn't do.

Freddie the cripple lurched over to the office. He circled it, poured gas in a thick path behind him. The pungent smell tickled his nose. He set the gas can down next to a tomato plant and dug into his pockets for a lighter. He'd need to find some paper around here, or maybe some dried bushes, but first he needed the flame to—

"Freddie? Is that you?"

Freddie the cripple rolled his eyes, took a deep breath. He turned around to face the writer.

The writer had a to-go cup of coffee in one hand, a white paper bag in the other. There was a screwed up look on his face, like what happens to a guy when he sees his paycheck on the Friday before Christmas.

Freddie the Cripple said, "You get a cinnamon roll?"

The writer glanced for a moment at the bag in his hand, licked his upper lip. "Almond croissant," he said. "There's a place just down the block and—"

"I bet you find yourself a wee bit confused."

"Yeah, Freddie. Ain't that the truth."

"The best I can say is, you got some enemies, brother."

The writer put the paper bag to his mouth, held it between his teeth as his hand patted the backside of his blue jeans. A second later, the writer flashed a small silver gun at Freddie the cripple. A pistol—

maybe a .25.

Freddie said, "A gun? Really?"

With the paper bag hanging from between his teeth, the writer somehow said, "You were about to commit arson. I got all my stories in there, motherfucker. That's my life's work. A gun? Yeah—I'm pointing a gun at you. What the fuck else did you expect?"

◊

In the back office of Yonder now, across town.

Freddie the Cripple taped to a rolling office chair, his arms starting to ache from the tight-as-shit duct tape around his wrists. The writer was sitting on the desk next to a clunker of a pc. He had that silver gun in one hand, tapped it lightly against the desk. His other hand was shoving the almond croissant into his mouth. He got it all the way in there and started chewing with loud grunts. The office was small and stuffy, packed with boxes of liquor and wine. Outside the closed door, Freddie heard the day bartenders hooting at each other, playing grab-ass before the lunch rush. He smiled at the writer. "Look, okay, this wasn't personal."

The writer finished chewing, swallowed the croissant with a huge gulp. "Sure it's personal. Not for you, maybe, but it's personal for somebody. The question is—who?"

That wiped Freddie's smile into oblivion. "Hey, look—I ain't never been a fucking snitch and I ain't never—"

The writer was up in an instant, his big left paw swinging at Freddie like the head of a sledgehammer. Freddie tried to duck, but the fist landed against his upper cheek bone and his head bounced against his shoulder. Someone was ringing the doorbell in his head. He groaned and fought fog in his eyeballs. "Christ, man...I swear you got a big punch."

The writer leaned back against the desk and sighed.

"I'd like to get this over with."

"Get what over with, man? You been making me margaritas for a week, maybe the best I ever had. Why you want to go and wreck that?"

The writer stood, used his right cowboy boot to kick Freddie the cripple in his gimpy leg.

"Ah! Fuck me, man!"

"Yeah—fuck the fuck out of you." The writer was down in Freddie's face, saliva peppering Freddie's cheeks as the words came at him like hail. "Fuck the fuck out of you for taking advantage of my kindness, for thinking you could fuck me without me knowing, and for hiding the identity of this prick who wants to ruin my work. Tell me who the fuck it is!"

"I can't, buddy."

"Is it Tommy! Ace! Is it Shawn? It better fucking not be Shawn. That ungrateful—"

"I can't say, man."

The writer punched Freddie the cripple in his balls. Freddie screamed like a little girl. He tried to hunch over, but found himself limited by the duct tape around his middle. His midsection felt like wet cement falling through a fishing net. "Good-fucking-god, buddy."

The writer pointed the gun at Freddie's balls. "You fucking tell me or I'm about to blow your ball sack through your asshole. I swear to the story gods from here to Timbuktu—I'll plug your cock through your kidney."

"Christ."

"I seriously doubt Christ had anything to do with this."

Freddie groaned, rested his chin against his sternum. "If I tell you, how the fuck am I ever—"

A loud pounding on the door. A woman's voice: "What the fuck are you doing in there? If you're going to be here, I need you to get out here and start on inventory with me!"

"Alright, give me a minute—just one fucking minute." The writer shook his head so hard that beads of sweat rained down on the back of Freddie's neck. "I need to handle this," he said to the closed door.

"I shouldn't tell you the guy's name, man. I really shouldn't. If I tell you then I'm never—"

"Freddie, let me ask you something."

Slowly, with great pause, Freddie the cripple lifted his head. "Go ahead."

The writer leaned down close to him. His eyes were bloodshot and angry. His lips peeled back into a sneer. "Do you want to know what it feels like when your dick pierces your own fucking kidney? Do you? Because if you do—"

"Fine, man." Freddie felt every thread of toughness in him unravel. He sagged like a damp cotton sheet. "I'll tell you. The guy who paid me, his name is—"

◊

Freddie the Cripple was on his third margarita. He was enjoying himself, shooting the shit with the writer. He rubbed his wrists, twisted every now and then to stretch his back. He was starting to feel better—about not getting his dick shot off and about not burning down the writer's office.

He liked this bar—Yonder.

Freddie the cripple said, "Why'd you open this place? I mean, shit, don't you got enough to do?"

The writer shrugged. "Yeah, there's plenty."

"These are some fucking good margaritas, but—"

"Tell you the truth…It's the stories. I like to be part of everybody's stories. I like to hear people tell stories. I like to tell stories myself. And, yeah, I make a decent fucking margarita. Call me crazy if you want, but—"

"Tell me something else," Freddie said. "The other writer, the guy who hired me—what are you going to do to him? How's that story going to end?"

The writer smiled and said, "The same way every good story ends— with somebody dead and in the ground. I'm going to give that mother-fucker what he deserves. But right now…I got a bar to run."

SARZARAC

Rye
Angostura
Peychaud's
Absinthe

"In this profession, it's a long walk between drinks."
– Truman Capote

Amounts have been left out. Live a little.

ERIC BEETNER
THE REGULAR

Gordon pulled on the door to Yonder Southern Cocktails and Brew and waited for his "Norm!" moment. The feeling of belonging someplace, of being a regular, like family. Instead he was slapped in the face by a high pitched laugh from somebody at the far end of the room and the smell of beer and someone who had overdone it on the Axe body spray. Nobody called his name.

No worries. Becoming a regular was a process, and Gordon had patience. He walked toward his regular barstool – second from the far end. Near the bartender, but not the last stool because that was just weird.

Gordon nodded to the bartender, the owner in fact, as Gordon had learned. Nice guy but looked a little dimwitted, like the kind of guy who didn't know how to properly spell his own name. But he was polite and pulled a great beer. Gordon gave him a smile and wave and the bartender gave him back a slight head nod, his hands wrist deep in washing some glasses.

There was a man on Gordon's stool.

He stopped, not quite sure what to do. The man was big. His wide back hunched over as he leaned both elbows on the bar and hovered above his beer bottle. He wore a denim work shirt, Timberlands, worn Dickies. Dark hair sprouted from his knuckles.

"You're...you're on my stool."

The guy didn't hear him or perhaps ignored him, so Gordon spoke a little louder.

"That's my stool."

The big man turned his head slowly as if it was made of heavy stone and took considerable effort to move. "Your what?"

"My stool. That's my regular seat."

The man turned his head back around to face the brick wall behind the bar. "Not tonight it ain't."

Gordon didn't know what to do. To be a regular you had to maintain a routine. Arrive at the same time every night. Sit in the same place. Make it so the bartender knew you. You became a part of his landscape, like the light fixtures and the exposed beams.

"But...that's my stool."

With a heavy sigh so thick it nearly tumbled to the ground with a thud, the big man turned again, this time rotating his body in a half turn to face Gordon.

"You can see I'm sitting on it, right?"

"Yeah, but it's just that it's my-"

"Yeah, yeah, I get it. It's your stool. Well, I just got here. This is my first beer, and I'm probably gonna have two to three, so find yourself another stool or find yourself another bar."

Gordon didn't want another bar. This one was new. No regulars yet. He could be the first. He'd be the one they talked about years from now. About how Gord showed up and always took that same stool. How he'd been there from the start.

Whenever anyone asked, which they hadn't yet but when they did, he'd say, "Call me Gord." Closer to Norm. Easy to shout when he walked in the door. Not simple, giving yourself a nickname, but with a new establishment like this he could start over. A new life. A new man. A regular.

"Look, buddy," Gordon said, "if you just move down one or two seats. Y'see, I'm a regular."

He gave a sheepish smile and a tilt of his head as if he was about to blush over his status as a Yonder regular. The big man was unimpressed.

The big man snapped his fingers twice and the bartender came over.

"Yeah?"

"This guy one of your regulars?" He pointed a thumb the size of a hot dog over his shoulder at Gordon.

The bartender/owner guy squinted at Gordon. Gord smiled, like let's get this over with and we can all move on and laugh about it years later. "I've seen him before, I think."

Gordon's face fell like he'd been stood up for the prom.

"He always sit on this stool?"

"Of course I do. It's Gord, you know me."

The big man spoke in a low rumble. "I wasn't asking you, Gord."

The bartender forced a smile. "Look, fellas, no need to for any trouble. Got plenty of seating and three dollar drafts tonight."

Gordon tried to stare a hole out through the man's back. "It won't be any trouble if this guy just moves."

"And why the hell should I do that?"

"Because that's my stool!"

Gordon's shout made every eye in the bar turn toward him. He felt his hands tremble with the dump of adrenaline his surge of anger had unleashed.

"Guys..." the bartender said.

"Move," Gordon said.

The big man took a slow sip from his bottle, set it down with a soft thunk, turned the stool with a scrape of the legs on the floor and said behind a hard stare, "No."

The bartender held out calming hands. "Hey, look, Bill it's not a big deal so–"

"You know his name?" Gordon roared.

The bartender looked confused for a moment, his hands reaching under the bar.

Gordon lowered his shoulder and charged. He knocked the big man, Bill, off the stool. Bill folded and got his bulk wedged between the last stool in line and the debated stool. Gordon reached up and snatched the beer bottle in his hand, upended it, spilling the last few sips onto the floor, and aimed the longneck at Bill's gaping mouth. Like a glass pacifier the neck of the beer went into Bill's mouth, chipping a few teeth on the way. Gordon torqued his wrist and the bottle snapped off, the broken glass of the neck filling Bill's mouth as blood began to seep from his shredded lips.

Behind Gord the bartender had come up from under the bar with a shotgun in both hands.

"That's enough of that."

Gordon shot his hands out like a whip crack, snagged the gun by the barrel and wrenched it from the bartender's hands.

"Think you'll remember me now?" His eyes showed white all around his irises. Tiny clouds of spittle collected in the corners of his mouth. He held the gun like a club, his knuckles going white with his grip.

The bartender threw his hands in the air and backed up until the bottles behind him in the rack shook and threatened to shatter as he bumped them. Then, in a flash, Gordon was gone. He went almost straight down, like a shark attack victim in a movie. His legs had been swept from under him and the only thing that kept him from going straight to the floor was his chin hammering against the bar top on his way down.

The solid crack of wood and bone was followed by a groan from the other patrons in the bar who all focused on the fight over the exclusive stool.

Bill stood over Gordon, blood leaking from his mouth in a steady drip. He picked up the shotgun, aimed it stock side down and pile drove it down into Gordon's face. Gord's nose flattened into mush.

Gordon wrapped two hands around one of Bill's Timberlands and twisted, his eyes shut with the pain and spattered blood from his broken nose. A sound like a tree limb snapping off in a storm filled the room and Bill howled in pain.

He tottered away, one foot wrenched ninety degrees the wrong way. Gordon pushed himself up on all fours.

The bartender had made his way around the bar and put a hand on each man's back to grab up a fistful of shirt and maybe get them out of the sidewalk and end this madness. Both Gordon and Bill swung fists into the bartender's gut. He coughed out all the air in his lungs and bent forward.

Gordon got hold of Bill's belt and hauled himself up, putting his bloody face inches away from Bill's. Bill, off balance on one good foot, spun and wrapped up Gord in a teetering waltz. They crashed into the bar, sending half full glasses of beer to the ground. The bar wasn't even, it zigged and zagged in and out like a mouth with missing teeth. The two headed beast spun and ricocheted off one of the protruding bar top sections and toppled over one of the less desirable bar stools.

"I'm a goddamn regular," Gordon slurred through blood and tears.

"Broke my goddamn ankle," Bill said.

"It's my stool."

"God dammit." The bartender stood, a feral animal look in his eye, teeth bared and the bar stool in question held up over his head. "My bar, my stool."

He brought it down and two of the four legs broke across Gordon's back. He released Bill and the bartender swung again, catching the big man across the chest with the remaining pieces of stool. The rest crumbled in his hands.

Both men hit the floor in a heap beside each other.

The bartender weaved a bit to get his balance, but he stood straight and looked over the two men.

"Now get out of my place."

Like two half-drunk tortoises the men crawled toward the door. The bartender leaned one elbow on the bar. He reached over and grabbed a bar towel and wiped his face.

Bill collapsed to the sidewalk out front, drooling blood. Gordon, behind him, stopped in the doorway on all fours. He turned back inside.

"See you tomorrow, same time?"

The bartender wiped his mouth with the towel, checked it for blood, exhaled deeply. "Sure thing, Gord. See you then."

MANGO MOJITO

Rum
Mango
Mint
Lime
Soda

"I hate to advocate drugs, alcohol, vio-lence, or insanity to anyone, but they've always worked for me."
– Hunter S. Thompson

Amounts have been left out. Live a little.

TODD MORR
SLAPPY SACRAMENTO

"Do I need to ask the puppet for I.D.?"

"It's not a puppet, it's a ventriloquist dummy."

"Oh, sorry."

The man in the fedora tapped his knuckles against the dummy's chest which was covered in a green plaid suit before he said, "He's made of wood."

"I know, it was just a joke..."

"The wood he was made from came from a three-hundred-year-old tree. They used to hang people from it back when that was the way we dealt with undesirables."

Jimmy wasn't sure how to respond to that.

The man knocked on the dummy again, "He's old enough to drink."

Jimmy smiled, "So, what can I get for him?"

"Nothing, he's a piece of fucking wood. You can, however, get me a Jack Daniels on the rocks."

"You got it," Jimmy told him before he went to grab a bottle off the shelf.

Carla returned to the bar after giving their only other customer a light beer. Unlike the man and his dummy, this guy sat didn't sit at the bar. He chose a high table in the corner and buried his face in his phone

Carla got close to Jimmy and spoke low, "Can I talk to you in the back?"

Jimmy nodded as filled a clean tumbler with ice before pouring some amber liquid over the cubes.

He set it in front of the man with the dummy and made his way to the back where Carla was waiting for him.

"You need to ask him to put that thing away," She told him.

"What thing?"

"The puppet."

"You mean the ventriloquist dummy?"

"Whatever. I just need it to be gone."

"Why? It's not hurting anybody."

"It's hurting me. That thing creeps me out."

"It's just a puppet and he seems to like it out, maybe it makes him feel like he has friends. We can't exactly be pissing off customers."

"Fine, but if he starts making it talk he's out of here."

"Just take care of the other customer and I'll handle him, okay?"

"Fine, just keep it away from me," Carla said as she stomped back into the barroom.

Jimmy shook his head. She was a good barmaid, nice to look at too but she had some issues. Jimmy returned to his post behind the bar

The man in the fedora sipped his drink and then picked up the dummy and put him on his lap.

"Slappy Sacramento," the stranger said.

"Excuse me?"

"My dummy's name. Slappy Sacramento."

"Oh."

The stranger sipped his whiskey again and shook his head, "This isn't Jack Daniels."

"Of course it is," Jimmy replied, "You saw me pour it right out of the bottle."

"The bottle says Jack Daniels and I'm sure at one time there was some genuine Lynchburg Tennessee whiskey in there but I'm guessing that was three of four bottles ago at best."

"I'm not going to say that kind of thing never happens but it never happens here. Yonder is a first-class drinking establishment."

"Don't be so defensive, I'm still drinking it. To be honest I would have been surprised if you actually had some Jack in that bottle."

"We may not be the fanciest place around but..."

"Who are you kidding bucko? This dump would need an upgrade to qualify as a dive. "

The man in the fedora's lips never moved. Slappy Sacramento's however, did.

Jimmy almost addressed the dummy before he caught himself. Instead, he looked at the man, "If you don't like it here you don't have to stay."

"Oh, I like it here fine. I've drunk enough whiskey to know the difference between Jack and Evan Williams but at the end of the day it's still a whiskey."

"Sure sounded like you were complaining before."

"I'm fine with it, Slappy, however, feels a little more strongly about it."

"The dummy?"

"Who you calling dummy bucko?"

Jimmy almost talked to the dummy but kept his focus on the man, "You trying to be funny?"

The man sipped his whiskey as Slappy said, "I asked you a question bucko. Who are you calling a dummy?"

Carla came around the bar stepped in front of the ventriloquist and his dummy. The dummy turned his head so his painted-on eyes were staring at her tits. She ignored the dummy and looked at Jimmy.

"I thought I made it clear. Didn't you hear what I said?"

Jimmy shrugged, "I heard you, but last I checked you worked for me not the other way around."

Carla glared at him long enough to make Jimmy uncomfortable before she turned to the ventriloquist and said, "If you're going to do that you're going to have to leave."

The dummy turned his head so he wasn't looking directly at her chest but his eyes went right back to her tits.

"I'm not talking about a block of wood looking at my boobs."

"Then what are you talking about toots?"

"You," Carla said as she pointed at the dummy, "We don't allow this kind of shit in our bar."

"Allow what kind of shit? Toots?"

"You damn well know what I'm talking about," she said to the dummy. She realized she was talking to a block of wood and turned her attention to the man in the Fedora, "Stop it."

"Stop what?" the dummy asked.

Jimmy got in the man's face, "If you don't stop with the dummy I'm going to have to ask you to leave?"

"Why?" the ventriloquist asked.

"Bar policy."

"You have a policy about ventriloquism?"

"We do now."

"Aw come on toots," the dummy said, "I'm not so bad if you get to know me."

Carla started to cry as she said, "Make it stop."

"I'm not going to ask you again…" Jimmy started to say.

"So you serve my friend here some bottom shelf coffin polish and then you throw us out of the bar? Hell of a way to do business there bucko," Slappy said as the ventriloquist stood up.

Carla grabbed the bottle of Jack off the shelves and shoved it in the dummy's face, "By the way, this is the real thing you piece of shit. This is an honest bar."

"Honest my wooden ass toots. I'm three hundred motherfucking years old. I know when someone is trying to pass off some firewater…"

Carla hit the dummy with the bottle. The bottle shattered covering the man in the fedora with whiskey. Slappy Sacramento's head went flying bouncing off the top of the bar and rolling under a table."

"What the hell lady?" the ventriloquist said, "Do you know how much he cost?"

"I told you to stop," Carla said as she shoved the jagged bottleneck still in her hand into his throat. She pulled it away and his severed jugular vein spurted out blood like a hose covering Carla in red sticky life fluid.

As the man in the fedora collapsed the young guy with the phone jumped out of his seat and went to the fallen ventriloquist.

"What the fuck lady?" he said as he stood over the dead man, "It was just a joke."

"A joke?"

"Yeah, we do a YouTube prank show," he said as he held up his phone to show he'd been filming the whole time, "we fuck with people and then put it on our channel but it's like all in fun."

"Well, you fucked with the wrong people," she told him as she hopped over the bar.

The young man realized too late that he should have been running the moment she stabbed the ventriloquist in the neck. He turned to go but she jumped on his back and started stabbing with the bloody bottleneck. She jabbed him in the face, neck, and chest before she started to ram the jagged glass through the top of his head. He made it a few steps with her on his back but soon the loss of blood and having someone jam broken glass repeatedly into his brain caused his legs to stop working.

They fell together and Carla stayed on his back, stabbing him repeatedly with the broken bottle.

Jimmy stepped around her and turned off the neon sign that said 'open' before he shut and locked the door.

"He's dead Carla."

Carla stopped stabbing him and looked up at Jimmy, "They shouldn't have done that."

"You can't keep doing this every time someone does something..."

"I hate ventriloquists."

"Yeah, I noticed," Jimmy said as he went to get the mop.

When he came out of the back room with the mop bucket Carla was stabbing the headless dummy in his wooden chest, making a mess of his plaid suit as she yelled, "Die motherfucker."

Carla was a great barmaid but she had some serious issues.

THE MOLOKO PUNCH

Vodka
Hazelnut
Creme de Cacao
Cream

*"There was me, that is Alex, and my three droogs,
that is Pete, Georgie, and Dim, and we sat in the
Korova Milk Bar trying to make up our rassodocks
what to do with the evening. The Korova Milk Bar
sold milkplus, milkplus vellocet or synthemesc or
drencrom, which is what we were drinking." – A
Clockwork Orange by Anthony Burgess*

Amounts have been left out. Live a little.

NICK KOLAKOWSKI
HUEY AND THE BURRITO OF DOOM

A s Huey leveled the .38 at the bartender, the gas-station burrito in his gut began to make its presence known.

Huey wasn't a professional criminal; in fact, you would have a hard time describing him as a professional anything. His last gig, as a Walmart sales associate, had ended after a spectacular incident involving a 48-ounce bottle of vegetable oil, a lighter, and a meth-crazed shoplifter. He was now banned from going within 100 yards of a Walmart, which rendered him shit out of luck with the county's largest employer—hence the pistol, the bar, and the words coming out of his mouth:

"All the money in the register. Now."

Huey figured that, at twenty minutes to closing time, the bar's cash register would hold at least a couple hundred bucks, right? Plus, at that hour, you usually had only a few diehard drinkers left—none of them happy to play hero, even if they could walk a straight line.

His low-watt brainpower didn't stop Huey from realizing the shoddiness of his plan, but what choice did he have? The rent on his trailer was three hundred bucks a month, and right now he had three dollars and fifty-one cents in his bank account. And a .38 with four bullets in it.

Staring into the barrel's abyss, the bartender smiled, seemingly unconcerned. Something about that smile made Huey's already-tortured stomach clench a bit harder. "There's not a lot in there," the bartender said, so calm he might have been ordering a double-cheeseburger.

"Don't care." Huey tried to sound as angry as he could, but thanks to the muscle-tightening effort required to keep the anal trumpet from sounding, it came out as an unmanly squeak. "You're gonna give it to me now."

"That's a nice costume," the bartender said, meaning the cheap clown mask strapped onto Huey's face. "Where'd you get it?"

"Money. Now." Huey stepped forward, bringing the barrel within an inch of the bartender's left eye.

The bartender didn't even flinch. Who was this badass? Huey had chosen to rob this bar, Yonder, because he never drank there—don't shit where you eat, as his mother always told him—and he was beginning to think that was a mistake. Shouldn't he have scoped the place out, maybe asked someone about it? If he still had a working phone, he could have checked a few reviews or something...

From the back of the bar, a new voice boomed, rough and loud and slurry with alcohol: "Gentlemen, this is a prime example of what we covered in class this afternoon."

Huey risked a glimpse in that direction, but it was impossible to detect shapes in the murk beyond the neon beer signs. He hadn't noticed anyone there when he walked in, but then again, he hadn't taken any time to look. Pumped on adrenaline and a shot of cheap whiskey, he had locked on the bartender from the first moment. Big mistake.

"Who's that?" Huey called, still doing his best to sound at least somewhat tough.

The door to the restrooms opened, ejecting a sliver of brightness that spotlit a large circular table. Around it sat five massive men in almost identical crewcuts, the sleeves of their t-shirts straining against massive biceps. One of these giants had a sandy moustache that looked like it belonged in a porn film from the Nixon years.

"Jimmy," said the Man with the Moustache, "what can you tell us about this situation here?"

"Well, that looks like a .38," said Jimmy, who sat to the left of the Man with the Moustache. "And it's hard to tell in this light, but it doesn't look all that well-maintained. Nonetheless, sir, as you told us in class, you always have to assume that a weapon is loaded, right?"

"That's right, Jimmy." The Man with the Moustache paused to sip his beer, then pointed at the house-sized dude emerging from the restroom. "Rick, what else can you tell us about this scene?"

"We know that Howard keeps a 12-gauge shotgun behind that bar, but the current position of the .38 makes reaching for it a dicey proposition." Rick gestured at the bar. "Sorry, Howard. Sort of spoiled your tactical advantage there."

"No worries," Howard the bartender said. "Wasn't thinking of reaching for it. Got other ways of dealing with this candy-ass."

"Hey." Huey felt offended. "I'm no candy-ass. I'm the one with the gun here, buddy."

Howard grinned. "Whatever you say, *buddy*. I'm not the one robbing a bar where *cops love to drink*."

Well, shit. The .38 barrel wavered as Huey absorbed that important bit of information. "Just give me the money," he said. "I'll get out of here. No need for this to turn into anything bad."

"Okay, group," said the Man with the Moustache. "The perp just said this wasn't 'bad.' What kind of criminal charges are potentially in play here?"

"Well, robbery..." Jimmy began.

The Man with the Moustache raised a hand. "Let's hear from someone new. Jill?"

"Possession of a deadly weapon, robbery, maybe assault?" Jill had the same crewcut as the rest, along with muscles that made her seem even larger than her companions—although maybe that was a trick of the light, plus the fear chemicals flooding Huey's cortex. "If you had an aggressive enough DA, plus some prior offenses, this gentleman is probably looking at ten, maybe fifteen years."

"Not even five, okay? Especially with good behavior." Huey tried to keep the cops—or student cops, whatever—and the ever-lovable Howard in his same field of view. "This isn't a big deal. Just give me the cash, okay? Please?"

"No," Howard said. "How about that? No. You can blow my head off, but I bet you don't make it three steps before the police in here splatter you all over the walls. They'll be picking dried bits of your skull out of the floorboards for the next five years..."

Huey's gut rumbled. He clenched the muscles around his rear exit as hard as he could, but that failed to fully stop the *basso profundo* fart barreling down the pike. Instead, his ass *whistled*, and Huey felt a piece of his soul crumble and die.

Why'd you go with the burrito? he thought miserably. Those things were probably warming on that gas-station rack for months, growing their own civilizations of bugs, and you couldn't have just bought a bag of chips, oh no, it was an important night and you *had* to go for the Mega Chicken with Black Bean—

The bartender waved a hand in front of his nose. "Holy shit, boy, what'd you eat? A dead squirrel?"

"Fine. I won't take the money." Keeping the .38 aimed at Howard's eye, Huey took a step back—his freshly humid underwear chafing his thighs as he did so. "Everybody goes back to just having their beers, okay?"

Jill's hand drifted beneath the table. "Sir? What now?"

The Man with the Moustache raised his eyebrows. "What did we learn the other week? The five principles of hostage negotiation? What was number one?"

"'Always give them a way out,'" the table recited, dutiful as a class of first graders running through their ABCs.

"And the way out is the door." The Man with the Moustache waggled his fingers at Huey. "Off you go. See you later."

"You let this scumbag leave," Howard said, "I'm gonna blow him away on general principles."

"You'll do no such thing." The Man with the Moustache shoved his chair back. For the first time, a hard note crept into his tone, promising pain, broken bones, holding cells that stank of bleach and piss. "I spend every day dealing with scum on the streets. I'm not really big on bringing my work into my favorite bar, okay? Don't worry, we're going to kick the almighty shit out of him, but we're not going to do it in here."

As the Man with the Moustache spoke, Huey retreated toward the door. Hey, he didn't make any money tonight, but he was alive, right? Once he was out of there, he could disappear. He knew all the country roads and forest lanes around there better than anyone, on account of driving around aimlessly for weeks after the Walmart thing.

There was an Amazon warehouse over by the state line, right? He could throw boxes around in a hundred-fifty-degree warehouse for twelve hours a day. No problem. Actually, that sounded worse than prison, but at least you got paid, right? Minimum wage sounded pretty good. He didn't need a lot to live on.

Shoving open the door, Huey disappeared into the dark.

And ran.

As he plunged through the night, he envisioned hordes of SWAT cops tearing after him. Helicopters rumbling overhead, satellites tracking his every move. Veering off the road, he plunged into the trash-strewn woods, chuckling in-between ragged gasps for breath. He had knocked off a cop bar. A cop bar! How wild was that?

All light dropped from the world. The foliage overhead blocked the stars. Huey slowed down, picking his way over roots and rotting logs. He stripped off the clown mask and tossed it away. Actually, he hadn't knocked off squat. 'Knocking off' something implied that you actually managed to get some money, and he had nothing.

His gut hurt again. That crappy burrito, still paying dividends. Well, at least he hadn't *shat* himself in that cop bar, right? Didn't that count as a victory in Huey World?

A burst of light through the trees. Headlights. A road up ahead—Winter Lane, right? He drifted in that direction, knowing that his trailer park was a mile or two beyond that.

He emerged from the undergrowth. A short, grassy incline led to the gravel shoulder. If he climbed that, crossed two lanes, then disappeared into the trees on the other side—he'd be home by three.

Another set of headlights, to his left. A flicker of blue and red. Cops.

Shit!

A crashing behind him, deep in the forest. He turned. Lights flickered between the trees. More cops, no doubt intent on hunting him down like an animal.

He could retreat to the trees, which might save him from the cops on the road, but not the cops in the woods. Maybe he could run across the road, risking those headlights spotting him? He didn't trust his luck after everything at the bar.

His gaze drifted to the left, locking on a storm drain belching mud into the grass. It looked tight, maybe too tight, but what other options did he have? He had spent his entire life in the crap, when you thought about it.

Breathing through his mouth, he backed into the storm drain, unwilling to plunge headfirst into stinking darkness. Twenty feet into the pipe, the opening was a circle of dim gray, barely discernable from the black around it. Flat on his belly, he felt his jeans filling with muddy runoff, cold at first but then... surprisingly warm, almost pleasant. He could stay in here forever—provided there weren't any rats.

And then, at that most excellent moment, he sensed another Hiroshima-caliber fart rolling down the pike. He clenched down, although he had no idea why; it's not like this pipe could reek any worse.

Shouting from outside, along with a screech of brakes. A flashlight played on the edges of the pipe. Huey held his breath.

"What you got?" A voice called. It sounded like Jill.

"Nothing," someone else yelled.

"So we keep going through the woods? Really?" Jill seemed

pissed. Huey felt a little sorry for ruining her evening, but he also felt the burrito-gas expanding him like a meat-balloon, and that was a far more pressing issue.

"No choice." It was a third person speaking now, maybe the Man with the Moustache. "What's a big rule of police work? Never let a suspect get away if we can help it, okay? Okay?"

Grunts of agreement. If Huey could hear those, the cops must be standing right around the pipe. What if they decided to check it out? Did he dare crawl deeper in?

"What about this pipe?" Jill asked, as if picking up on Huey's thoughts over the air.

"Too small for that fat-ass in the bar," someone called from the road.

Well, excuse me all to hell, Huey thought. The gas was painful now, making him wince, and so he clamped harder, praying that his body would obey his mind for once—

"Well, let's keep moving," said the Man with the Moustache. "We'll also put out an APB. We'll get him."

Good luck with that, Huey thought. An APB for Clown Face.

"Yeah, let's go," Jill said. "And when we do find this guy, I got dibs on the plunger, got me?"

We'll see about that, Huey wanted to yell. We'll just see! For the first time in my life, I'm about to get away with something, and it feels glorious. Hey, maybe I should apply to Walmart again—with a lucky streak like this, I might even get my old job back. I bet they've cleaned up all that fire damage by now.

Like a greased rat shooting through a funnel, his fart escaped. Actually, 'escaped' was too weak a term. In that tight metal tube, the fart was a shotgun blast from hell. It seemed to shake the world itself.

White light blinded him. He tossed the .38 aside and raised his hands.

"The sad thing is," Jill said, her voice echoing down the tunnel, "you haven't even hit rock bottom yet. You might think you have, but you haven't. You got so much room to fall, you dumb asshole."

Huey let his head dip until his forehead touched the muddy run-off, his rear loosing a final, forlorn toot as he yelled: "How does it get *worse*?"

LAZY SUNSET

Tequila
Triple Sec
Blueberry
Pomegranite

Speaks well of a man to need a little something in this world. I wouldn't trust a man who could git through it cold sober.
— *Harry Crews*

Amounts have been left out. Live a little.

ALLISON A. DAVIS
THE DOOR IN THE FLOOR

T he bartender noticed her as soon as she came through the door, the light behind her creating a silhouette within the dark bar. She moved toward him, and he felt her in the room, as if she filled it up. Her dress fit her flawlessly, flowered and sleeveless, matching the warm, late summer day. Her figure was perfectly proportioned, and her legs, attractive, curved with muscles. She was taller than most women, and her hair bounced around her shoulders as if a wind blew.

Late afternoon light danced around the few patrons that would show up for an afternoon beer before happy hour. Music stands and microphones left over from the night before stood, skeletons of music past, awaiting the future of more live music that night.

He nodded at her, and he knew she noticed his eyes going up and down. Well, who wouldn't? It was a nice body.

"What'll ya have?" he said. He smiled, but felt it fall off her like a shedding leaf. She wasn't going to warm up quickly.

"Daiquiri. Old school. Up."

She didn't seem like the kind that drank that kind of drink. "Uh, one of these?" He pointed to the ice machine.

"You must not be the regular bartender."

He wasn't sure what she meant. Did she mean Pruitt? He had never seen her before, what did that mean? What would she know about Yonder?

She kept at him, standing at the bar. The leather backpack slung over her shoulder was unzipped.

"I said up."

She doubled down on him. "A real daiquiri is fresh lime juice, simple syrup and rum, shaken and served up. Do you think you can handle that?"

He hadn't known he could blush, but he felt put down by that simple statement, as if he'd been strong-armed to a kneeling position.

"Yes ma'am. Coming right up." He'd figure out how to engage her after he got a couple drinks in her. From her accent, he could tell she wasn't from North Carolina. Ordering hard liquor middle of the afternoon, who'd she think she was, coming in here, acting like a regular?

The woman pulled out an iPhone, sat at the bar and thumbed through it. Her backpack pulled her dress askew.

He held a squeeze bottle with lime juice over a measure and glanced at her over the stainless-steel shaker. She raised her eyebrows. "Is that fresh?"

"Squeezed it myself this morning."

That didn't seem to impress her. She went back to her phone.

He set down a round coaster with a local brewer featured, Regulator Brewing, and put a perfect daiquiri in front of the woman. She didn't even look up. Bitch. What is up with that? After all her complaining?

Her hand moved from her phone to the bar and she carefully carried the glass to her lips to take a sip while reading the screen. She licked her lips.

"Not bad," she said flicking him a look.

He nodded at her with a smile he wasn't feeling. How was I going to make it any better? There was only one way to make them, and it's pretty simple.

He moved down the bar to serve Jake and Max, two regulars. They both swung their eyes over at the woman, as if to ask him what was up with her? He shrugged and refilled their pint glasses.

"So tell me, what was your name again?"

He hadn't told her. "Brett. What's yours?"

"Brett." She nodded. "You used to work at the Texaco in downtown Durham before you got hired to work here at Yonder, right?"

She was right, but her knowing about him made him queasy.

"And your daddy left when you were nine, and your mama has worked at the dollar store ever since." Her smug smile made him angry. She said mama like a Southern girl, but without the accent.

She was scaring him now, and he didn't want to ask her any questions. He wanted her to shut up and leave. He needed to know though. "So, who you been talking to, anyway?

She ignored his question again, and he was starting to get pissed off.

Just then the phone rang and he answered. "Yonder, Southern Cocktails and Brew."

"Oh. Eryk," he turned from the bar so the woman couldn't overhear him. "There's a woman here and she seems to know a lot about the bar, and she asked about you. You expecting someone? I dunno, she's not from around here, but maybe-, ah hell, I don't know a woman's age, older than my sister, younger than my mama. You get my drift?"

"Yeah, sure."

Brett glanced over his shoulder at the woman. Her glass was empty. Maybe he'd make her another drink on the house, get more info from her. He could see a white envelope sticking out of her bag, and it worried him.

"You want another one of those?" he nodded at her empty glass.

"No, I'm good. How about some water?"

No more drinks, eh? Why she was here he could guess. He filled a pint glass with ice and water.

**

Eryk walked into the bar, looking around and spotted the woman that Brett had described on the phone sitting at the bar, to the left. He noticed her dress, sleeveless with arms that worked out, a short skirt showing taut and curvy legs, looking great, and relaxed.

Her back straightened as he moved in, but he hadn't said anything. As he approached the bar, she turned out of her seat and faced him in one movement.

He had never seen her before as he ran his eyes over her body and liked what he saw.

"How d'ya do? I'm…"

She interrupted him. "Eryk Pruitt? One of the owners of Yonder?" Her hands were out as if showing off the bar and she turned her head from side to side as if to take in the breadth of it.

"Why yes I am. And who are you? And did you bring snacks?"

She stopped a moment, and then started up again. "My name is Susan Mercer, and I've been vested with the power…"

He didn't let her finish her speech. He figured it out and started to back out of the door.

With that, everything started to move fast. She was up, her right arm going into her pack.

As Eryk reached the door, she drew out a .357 snub nose, shiny bright and held it steady in her hand. "You might want to stay," was all she said.

Eryk couldn't see what she held, but rather sensed that his back was exposed and froze. The entire room was stock still, a tableau. All eyes on the door.

Pruitt's hands went up. "What do you want?"

"You," she said, pulling handcuffs out of her bag.

"What the hell…" Brett came out from around the bar.

The woman pivoted to the back wall where she could keep an eye on the entire bar, and her gun on Eryk and Brett. "Stay back, this doesn't concern you."

"Doesn't concern me? He's my boss."

"Right now, he's going to go back and he knows why."

Eryk was quiet, and his hands were getting tired. He was resigned, his body sagged. He knew what was coming.

He turned back towards the bar. "Ok, you got me."

Brett was confused, looking from Eryk to the woman, who still held the gun on Eryk but her arm sagged as she started to move towards him with the handcuffs.

Eryk then turned, rushed the woman, hitting her in the chest with his elbow hard, and she fell, but didn't let go of the gun and didn't stay down.

Eryk then ducked behind the bar, a yawning sound and a slam. Brett ran back to follow him, a little afraid of the fun. Another door slammed.

Now she was up on her feet and her gun out, she slowly turned towards the bar. The gun was now fixed on Brett. "Where is he?"

Brett stared at her. Others in the bar, including Jake and Max, continued to watch as if it were a play going on in situ – and they were all its actors. No one moved.

She came around the edge of the bar and looked down at the floor, where a large hole in the floor revealed stairs that descended into inky blackness. She glanced down at the hole and back up at Brett who stood on the other side of the entrance. "He go down there?"

Brett shrugged, still unable to move. The woman hesitated and pointed down the stairs. "Where do these go?"

"Uh," Brett stammered. "Used to be part of the underground railroad, you know? Where folks could hide, and then there's a tunnel…" Brett's eyebrows went up and he shrugged.

"You hiding him on purpose?" Her voice was icy calm and gave Brett the willies.

Brett kept looking at her, not responding. She waved her gun at him, but he remained unmoved, betting she wasn't going to shoot him.

She glanced around, hesitating. "Where does it come out?"

Brett shrugged again. "Not sure now, what is actually open. There used to be multiple exits, but I don't know what works. I don't go down there."

She took a breath, pulled out her phone and turned on the flashlight, and went down the stairs.

Brett stood still, music playing in the background, "30 days in the Hole" by Humble Pie. One of the regulars, Clint, came up. Brett hadn't noticed him sitting over by the couch. "Maybe I'll get a pilsner?" The atmosphere in the bar was hushed.

"Sure, hang on a second." Brett hauled up the door, shut and locked it. He rolled the rubber mat back over it, got a pint glass, and poured a beer. After setting it on the bar and taking Clint's money, he walked over to the supply closet and opened the door. "She's gone now."

Eryk walked out of the supply closet.

"I gotta get that warrant fixed. Someone wants that bail money."

Brett nodded. "Yeah, it's going to get crowded down there eventually."

Pruitt nodded. "Guess I'll go set up for the music tonight."

"Might want it pretty loud," said Brett.

"Oh, and Brett."

"Yeah?"

"We don't serve daiquiris, never have."

"Got it."

CAIN TUCK MULE

Bourbon
Lime
Ginger Beer

"You are dehydrated. The result of alcohol taken to excess. But that is the only way to take it. It is the only way to do a man any good."
– Robert Penn Warren

Amounts have been left out. Live a little.

JUDY WILKINSON
CLOSE YOUR LAPTOP

I'm not even sure if I should be sharing this here, but after a few sleepless nights, and long days of being numb, scared and confused, I just feel like I need to let someone know what's going on, and hopefully find help.

About a month ago, I started dating this guy I met through a friend. I'd been single for some time, and just hadn't had any luck in hitting it off with someone, beyond a date or two. To say I wasn't optimistic this time around, would be a bit of an understatement. But something about this guy... I don't know... just grabbed my attention.

Who am I kidding? I know exactly what it was. He was so warm, and safe. He felt like coming home. I could see the inquisitiveness in his eyes, and feel the comfort in his hands.

His charm and smile announced the type of life he had lived. The crinkles in his eyes, and the subtle laugh lines that framed his mouth, explained in great detail the places he'd been, and the exciting things he'd done. The way he told stories, made me feel like I'd been by his side the entire time, and the way he listened made me feel like I was the most captivating person he'd ever laid eyes on.

Looking back, it was sickening. During it, it was sickening, but I didn't want to see.

He seemed like the type of person I could spend all of my time with, whether laughing, or in perfect silence. Despite this week's past events, a small, insane, part of me still wants to believe he's that sweet guy laughing at videos with me. One of the main things I should mention, was his fascinating collection of tattoos. There was one in particular that stuck out to me. A bar code.

He just laughed it off, and claimed that it was the result of some stupid dare. He said that he and some friends thought they would get barcodes of things like "pound cake" or "red bull". He said it was probably the worst decision he's ever made, but he assured me that it was all in harmless fun. Then, like a flash of lightning, the moment passed.

Our adventurous date nights turned into lazy Sunday mornings, and then into long weekends, until each day began to meld together. Ignorance was bliss. One night, after we had finished fooling around, he suggested that we try something a little more adventurous. Since I'd been feeling happier than ever, I agreed to hear him out. He asked how I felt about BDSM. Hesitantly, I told him that we should start slow, since that was something I'd never even imagined exploring at the time. Thankfully he understood, and told me that we could take it as slow as I wanted, which was a huge relief.

The next day, I decided to take a look online at some videos just to get the feel of it, and see if I could find anything I'd like to try for a start. At first, it was pretty vanilla, just with a few sprinkles. Black sprinkles, with whips and chains. I was a little stunned at first, but slowly found myself intrigued by certain aspects. After an hour of browsing, I came across something much more sinister.

The video started off with a woman bound to a contraption of a chair in a dimly lit room, with the look on her face that resembled that of a frightened animal.

Something wasn't right, this seemed far too real. She didn't have the same enthusiasm as the women from the other videos, or tears streaming down her face. She just looked empty, as if she had no more tears to cry. Just a scared. empty. shell.

Curiosity, fear, and concern gripped me by the shoulders. I wanted to stop watching, but I couldn't. Four men appeared from the shadows each with a whip in hand. They beat her until she was covered in scars across her face, her arms, anywhere they could get to. There was a pool of blood down by her feet, and she had the most chilling glazed over look. An additional group of men in black cloaks appeared. Eventually, I realized that whatever I was watching, had some sort of ongoing chat.

At first, I thought it was those pop up ads, but no, they seemed to be real people, encouraging this poor woman's torment. I was shaking in my seat as I read the chat. I felt as if I was going to vomit. They removed the gag in her mouth for a moment, and I could have sworn I saw her say, "help me."

Surely, this wasn't what he was thinking of trying with me. I was scanning the room in the video to see if I could find any clues as to where the woman was located, when the light began to focus on her, and a few men close by. In the shadows, I saw more obscure figures wearing masks, just silently watching.

I can't bring myself to even type the things that began to happen to that poor girl. I have no idea what I'd hoped to accomplish by tossing my two cents into the chat room, but for whatever reason, I shakily typed out, YOU PEOPLE ARE SICK. Now, I wish that I never had.

One of the men beating the woman pulled off his shirt, and there it was across his chest. A bar code. One not too different from the one on the man who was just in my bed last night...

Chills tumbled down my spine, and spread across me, paralyzing my hands and legs. I just wanted to stop watching.

Then I glanced down and saw a message in chat that read,

"Hello beautiful, do you like what you see?"

I wasn't sure what to do at that point. My mind raced to find an explanation. There was no way that could be him.

My phone rang. It was him calling me.

"Hey I need to know what you are doing right now."

I stuttered incoherently, "oh um, nothing much just cleaning some." I knew it was him, but that wasn't the voice of the man I'd spent the last two months with. I held back tears, as I saw my inbox get flooded with more, and more vulgar, and malicious messages. I felt like these men knew me. They began to describe what they would do to me, right now, or if they found me on a street late at night. Then, they began to describe my living room, my bedroom, and most unsettling of all, what I was wearing.

After a few moments, his voice pierced my thoughts, as I heard him say,

"Close your laptop, close it now."

It sickens me when I think about his voice now. Then I heard him calmly repeat, "I said, close it. listen to me. Don't ask me questions right now, just do it." I did, but it was too late. I saw them pour gasoline on a limp, and ravaged woman, then casually toss a match at her feet. I saw the lights go out, and the men leave the room, as if they'd simply just finished watching a film. I sat there broken, as if I my body had just fallen off of 40 stories.

I couldn't comprehend what was happening. It didn't seem real. It still doesn't, but I know it was. I had just watched a woman get murdered. I knew he hadn't been in that room, but I also knew he... Well, now I don't know what I thought I knew. I had so many questions, so many worries. I sobbed into the phone, "What the hell? Who the fuck are you?!" I hung up before he had a chance to answer.

The next few days were pure agony, and why I've broken down and decided to share this here. He showed up yesterday. I hadn't slept the entire night, but I'd calmed down as much possible. I expected lies, an explanation, or compassion at least. However, all I was met with, were 6 words. **Do NOT go to the cops.**

I stood there stunned. He kissed me on the forehead and left. I've called out of work for the past two days.

I'm afraid to leave my house, because I think I'll only to come home, and find someone waiting for me. I'm afraid of uncovering the camera on my laptop, because I have no idea who, or what is watching me now. That woman's face haunts me. I hear things at night. I'm tired. I'm afraid to sleep, because I might wake up with someone over my bed, or wake up in a room full of men I don't know. I'm afraid of uncovering the camera on my laptop, because I have no idea who, or what is watching me now, where they're watching me from, or how long it'll be before they find another way to see me again.

HEMINGWAY DAQUIRI

Rum
Grapefruit
Lime
Luxardo

"The daiquiri, so well beaten as it is, looks like the sea where the wave falls away from the bow of a ship when she is doing thirty knots."
– Ernest Hemingway

Amounts have been left out. Live a little.

S.A. COSBY

THEY HAVE FANCY DRINKS NAMED AFTER FAMOUS WRITERS

S kunk sat in the corner of the bar sipping a Jameson on the rocks with the grim determination of a badger chewing its own leg off in a trap. Darlene was sitting at the bar proper in a skirt so short it looked like a belt. She checked her watch and Skunk silently chided her for it.

BootLip sat in a beanbag near a sand pit in the middle of the bar. Darlene's friend, a tall drink of water from East Texas now residing in North Carolina, said it was a bocce ball pit.

Skunk didn't know what bocce ball was but he figured it was something people who wanted to think they were cool played without keeping score.

Darlene checked her watch again.

Skunk choked down the Jameson. He preferred rye but the bartender, Mr. East Texas, said they were all out of rye so Jameson it was. Skunk caught Darlene's eye and she nodded towards the door. He nodded curtly. The pimp was going to show. BootLip, posing as a rich old pervert, had promised him 10k for Darlene's little sister.

Guys like that were drawn to money like flies to shit. The pimp would show up, BootLip would show him a dummy roll. Ten stacks of one-dollar bills with a hundred-dollar bill on top in duffle bag. Then they would take him in the back and beat the living shit out of him until he told them where he was keeping Darlene's little sister.

The pimp liked to talk tough. Tell anybody who would listen that he used to run with the Hell's Angels. Talk about a man he'd killed who had stepped on his shoes. Talk about how he once beat a guy in a bare-knuckled fight then won 25k by betting on himself. Talk about how he had once fucked Barbara Mandrell.

Talk, talk, talk.

In Skunk's experience it was the ones who talked the most who broke the quickest. Break one of their fingers and they'd confess to the Lindbergh kidnapping. Pull their left nut off with a pair of pliers and they'll confess their mama was in on it.

Skunk sipped the Jameson again. He watched Darlene throw back a shot of something. Her dark brown hair was hidden under a long red wig and a battered Yankees baseball cap. She'd called him a week ago, her voice trembling with rage.

"Three days ago, I come home from the club to find a note on the fridge. It's from Julie telling me she done ran off with the love her life. Right. She's six-fucking-teen. She knows about as much about love as a monkey knows about flying a plane. I figure she'll cool off in a week or two and come slinking back to her big sister's house with her tail between her legs and her cherry popped. Then a regular pulls me aside tonight after I get off stage. He's seen Julie waiting for me around the club more than once. He's tells me he was on the internet scrolling through some pay for play sight and he's sees a girl he swears is Julie. Says he recognizes the rose tattoo I gave her on her left arm. I go and check out the site. It's her, Skunk. Some prick has my little sister selling ass for fifty bucks a hit. "

Skunk had met Darlene when he'd been in Norfolk, VA, collecting a debt for Chuly Pettigrew. It had been a nasty piece of work that had ended with a hammer, a shovel and a hacksaw.

"You know the guy she ran off with?" Skunk asked.

"Yeah but it's gotta be a nickname. I went through her Facebook and saw some guy named Bullet talking her up. Telling her how much he loved her, how sexy she was. Sexy. Right. Up to three months ago she was sleeping with a fucking night light." Darlene's voice had cracked then.

"Skunk you think you can ask around? Maybe find something out about this guy?" She said. The pauses between her words told him she was crying but she was trying to hide it.

"Yeah."

So, he'd asked around. He'd found out that Brian "Bullet" Thomas was a wannabe tough guy and a full-time pimp. No one knew where he stayed for sure but they knew he was in the Durham area.

"I can go by some places he might be hanging out. Follow him home. Grab Julie and bring her back if you want." Skunk had told Darlene a week later.

"By that time, she'll be worn out or he might have sold her to some fat fuck with heavy pockets," she'd said. An idea materialized in Skunk's head.

"What if we was the fat fucks?"

And that was how they'd found themselves in Yonder Bar on King Street in downtown Hillsborough, NC, waiting on a piece of shit with a couple of fake Hell's Angel's ta65ttoos that were just different enough from the real death's head to keep him from getting his arm's set ablaze. Darlene's regular, a fat trucker who called himself BootLip

155

was playing the rich pervert. Skunk thought the way he followed Darlene around he should change his name to NoseWideOpen.

Skunk motioned at the bartender. The tall Texan came walking over. Skunk hadn't asked how he and Darlene knew each other but they must have been tight. He was letting them commit six or seven different felonies in his bar. The Texan slipped through the tables and the stools and bean bags with a loose-limbed agility that made Skunk think he was probably good in a fight or a dance off.

"Want another?" The Texan asked.

"I'd rather drink Donkey Piss." Skunk said.

"I think that's an IPA." The Texan said. He smiled. Skunk didn't smile back. He curled his finger and the Texan bent forward.

"When Bullet gets here if those two at the end of the bar are still here get rid of them." Skunk whispered in his ear.

"David and Wendy? They'll be gone in a few."

"Good." Skunk said. The Texan straightened but he didn't go back to the bar. He was fidgeting he was holding back a river of piss.

"Yeah?" Skunk said.

"I hope you don't get upset but I was curious. I'm figuring they call you Skunk because of the white stripe. But I was just wondering…." He trailed off.

"How'd I get it?" Skunk offered.

"I guess I ain't the first person to ask you that." The Texan said. Skunk shrugged. His leather jacket shifted on his narrow shoulders.

"Nah you ain't." Skunk said. He stared at the Texan with his ice blue gunslinger eyes. The Texan nodded.

"Duly noted. "He said and headed back to the bar.

Another hour passed and Skunk was starting to second guess himself with a short stocky guy walked into the bar wearing a black muscle shirt with sparse amounts of actual muscle. He had a dirty blonde mullet that was thinning on the top but a raging party in the back. He scanned the bar with a pair of muddy brown eyes that made Skunk think of a rat. Those rodent-like eyes settled on BootLip in his thrift store suit. The stocky guy made a beeline for him.

"Reinhold?" Bullet asked as he stood in front of BootLIp.

"That's right. Are you Mr. Bullet?" BootLIp said with an unmistakable coastal Virginia drawl. Bullet pulled a chair over to the bean bag and sat in front of BootLip.

"Pull your shirt up. "Bullet said.

"I'm sorry?" BootLip said.

"I didn't stutter, son. Pull your shirt up. Not for nothing but I don't know you and I ain't trying to end up facedown on the sidewalk with bracelets on so let's make sure you ain't wired up." Bullet said. BootLip leaned back in the bean bag and opened his vest and pulled up his shirt. He exposed a big but firm hairy belly.

"Satisfied?" BootLip asked?

"Like a new wife on her wedding night." Bullet said. Skunk wasn't sure if he was being sarcastic or not.

"You got the money?" Bullet asked.

"Where's the merchandise?" BootLip asked?

"You primed up huh? I'll tell you she's a tight little piece. I really hate to lose her." Bullet said. Skunk couldn't see his face but he would have bet dollars to donuts he was smiling.

"I just want to make sure you ain't wasting my time," BootLip said. Skunk nodded at Darlene. She turned to the Texan and nodded. The Texan made his way to the front door.

Just as he was about to lock it, Julie walked in. Darlene jumped up so fast her hat fell off her head.

"Julie!"

Julie took one look at her sister then screamed.

"Baby it's a set up!"

"You motherfucker!" Bullet said. He jumped up eyeing the door.

Skunk got up and crossed the room in two steps. He pulled a .357 from his waistband and put the barrel behind Bullet's ear.

"Slow your roll Hoss. "Skunk said. Bullet froze. Darlene rushed toward Julie but her sister juked her and ran at BootLIp. She produced a pocketknife out of thin air and held it against BootLIp's neck.

"Let...let him go." Julie said.

"Julie this piece of shit had you online selling your ass. He don't care about you." Darlene said.

"Shut up. Bullet loves me! You're the one who doesn't care. I heard you say you were sick of having me in your house. It ain't even a house; it's a trailer Darlene!" Skunk glanced at Darlene. Darlene looked down at the floor.

"Look I did say that but that was just because it's been hard since Mom died. She was never a real mother to us so I wasn't sure I could be a mom to you. I only said that because we had been fighting earlier. And we was only fighting because I was worried about you. Now please put the knife down." Darlene said.

"NO! Bullet said you'd say some shit like that. He's the only one who actually wants me around." Julie said. Skunk shook his head.

"What you wanna do here Darlene? Because I'm about five seconds away from ending this." Skunk said. His gravelly voice sounded especially raspy after downing that Jameson.

"Um we just had that floor put in. Just saying." The Texan said.

The lights in the bar were low and sallow. Yet Skunk see the toll all this was taking on Darlene. Her face was drawn as tight as the skin on a baseball.

"If we give you the money will you leave her alone?" Darlene asked. Her voice was as flat as day old beer. Skunk could see all the fight had gone out of her like water in leaking out a rusty bucket.

"It ain't about the money, Darlene." Julie said.

"All of it?" Bullet asked.

No one spoke for a few long seconds.

"Yeah. All of it." Darlene said finally. Bullet made a show of thinking it over. The show closed quicker than Spiderman on Broadway.

"Okay sure." Bullet said.

"Let him go, Skunk." Darlene said. Skunk put the .357 back in his waistband. Julie stepped away from BootLip. The older man grabbed the duffle bag next to the bean bag and handed it to Bullet. Bullet walked around BootLip and headed for the door. Julie started to follow him; a ten-kilowatt smile etched on her face.

"Hey you heard your sister. She just paid 25 thousand to take you home to your shitty trailer." Bullet said. Julie stopped in her tracks.

"What? What are you saying Bullet?" She asked. Her big eyes widened to the size of fifty cent pieces.

"What am I saying? Jesus you're fucking dumber than I thought. This is enough for me to get out a town. Maybe head out West and get me nice first string of girls. Don't get me wrong honey you're tight as a drum but when it comes to fucking you know about as much about as I know about brain surgery." Bullet said.

"But..I did things for you. To you! You told me I was your special girl."

Bullet laughed. It was braying howl.

"What can I say? You just graduated from the school of hard knocks Magna Cum Load." He said. He started laughing even harder at his own joke.

"Damn that's cold blooded," the Texan said. Skunk almost shot Bullet right then on general principles. But maybe this was a hard lesson Julie needed to learn.

Julie stood there in front of Bullet as he laughed and laughed. Darlene moved toward her. She might have been planning to put her arms around her sister. Whatever she had been planning went out the window two seconds later.

Julie took the pocket knife and plunged it into the side of Bullet's neck the laughter died immediately. Bullet stumbled, fell into the bar then slid to the floor. He was still holding the duffle bag in his right hand. He seemed like he wanted to pull the knife out with his left but he couldn't make it carry out his wishes.

"You …. fucking…bi………" Bullet said. As lasts words go they weren't great but also not totally unexpected.

"Julie what did you do!?" Darlene said. She grabbed Julie by the shoulders and spun her around. Tears like streaks of melted snow ran down her cheeks.

"He made me do things, D. He made me do nasty things." She said. A guttural moan escaped Darlene's throat. She pulled Julie in tight and wrapped her arms around her.

"Should we…uh call the cops?" The Texan asked.

"Eryk, we can't call the fucking cops. Everybody in here except for you is either running from warrants or has just killed someone." Darlene said.

"I've done both." Skunk said.

"Well shit, D, I mean, I like you and all but there's a fucking dead body on my new floor. Jesus H. Christ buttercup!" Eryk said.

Skunk looked at Bullet's rapidly cooling body. Then he looked at the bocce ball pit. Then back at Bullet.

"Hey Eryk. You got a hacksaw?" Skunk asked.

THE GHOST WRITER
(NON-ALCOHOLIC)

Black Currant Nectar
Southern Sweet Tea
Ginger Beer

"Everything in moderation, including moderation."
– Oscar Wilde

Amounts have been left out. Live a little.

LIAM SWEENY
LEGS DIAMOND

That section of West King Street was an August wind-tunnel, pushing through damp air that set on everyone's skin like clumps of fresh-boiled cotton. Rory's glasses split the river of sweat coming from his forehead into tributaries that stained their courses on his cheeks. He was sick. His allergy was kicking up. Then again everyone was allergic to high-test bourbon and deep-fried salt-and-vinegar chips in that heat.

Eryk gave him refuge in the back room earlier to let him sleep before his shift. Rory would be sure to pay Eryk a little rent during happy hour. He wouldn't have minded renting a couch in Yonder, considering how half his day was spent making repairs on the property. But dipping hands into cookie jars and playing conflicts of interest would renew his membership in the "deadbeat dad" club.

So she got her check every week and he lifted, and pushed, and wired his way into a studio apartment above a mom-and-pop hardware store on the outskirts of Durham, one that he'd see more of if the music wasn't so good at Yonder come eight o'clock. But oh good, sweet bobble-head-swinging Jesus it was.

Not that it was love at first sight. When he first walked up to the brick-face building, he saw the paint chipping on ornate wrought-iron benches that filled the concrete front where other businesses might have wanted flower-pots. It was a new building for Coulson Property Management, and Rory got it because his boss figured that sooner or later he would get himself in enough shit to justify a clean boot. And Rory was a drunk, not an idiot, and he knew Yonder was the closest thing his boss could come to a "honey trap."

Rory walked around the corner of West King to the parking lot with a sledgehammer, his pulse pounding through his palm into the rough wooden handle. He would've hired some kid to break concrete that day if he planned on staying sober that night, but two-for-one specials were better than aspirin, so he'd grit his teeth a little.

They had a concrete company coming to replace a few slabs, and his boss, cheap dick that he was, figured he only really had to pay trade prices for the pouring. So he gave Rory a sledgehammer and a box of contractor bags. The sun was just past high noon. The concrete would well be hot by then. Rory didn't know if the chunks would melt the bags enough to rip through.

Eryk was outside when he got there, spraying the slabs with a hose he had coiled up on the outside wall.

"Shit'll dust up on ya' otherwise," he said.

"You are a true gentleman."

Eryk turned the hose on his hand, forming a grip as he rinsed it.

"You looked like puked-up dog shit, my man," he said. "I can fix you up a couple of bottles of water, no charge, just drink 'em up. What say?"

Rory nodded as he set the contractor bags down and wiped off his forehead. "I could use a shot too, if you're feeling generous."

"I don't think a shot'll treat you too good in this heat. But the waters, I'll go grab those." Eryk dipped into the back door and left it open a crack. Rory sighed and picked up the sledgehammer.

Eryk popped out occasionally as Rory bashed the center slab. He was bashing his head in unison with the pulverized aggregate and cement. He weighed throwing up where he stood against the fact that his bile would only mix with the dust and form a whole new type of cement.

Instead he put himself far away, to Charlotte in the fall of five years prior. Samuel, his smile broken by a dance along cinderblocks on the one time his mother got caught unawares, was downer than a down kid could be. Two of his top teeth were out, and he was stuck on baby food for a month while the surgery they did on his jaws healed. But sure as shit, Rory walked in from work with two teeth, the same two teeth, blacked out with a Sharpie's marker. And in his arms was enough baby food for a month – for both of them.

It was the best of Rory's memories. It was the first time Rory looked good to his own kid. They shared more than a look or a diet; they were in something together. He didn't take an ounce of pleasure in the fact that they were excluding Lilly; he even tried to get her on the baby food diet. It was about so much more. Rory went there often when he was slumming it behind a dumpster.

Rory had the center slab completely broken up before he stopped for a break. He leaned against the back wall and sunk down, sliding to rest his ass on an unfurled contractor's bag. He grabbed one of the waters out of the bucket Eryk set out, swirled it around the half-melted ice and brought it to the pulse in his neck. His frame sunk under the relief and he twisted of the top and took it down in gulps known only to the most ardent beer guzzler.

"Hit's the spot, don't it?" Rory didn't hear Eryk come out.

"Thanks, man. I needed this shit."

Eryk walked to the edge of the broken-up slab and kicked it

around with his foot.

"Reckon I'm gonna have footprints on it, soon as they pour it."

"Bet that fat fuck Barry will do it just for braggin'."

"I will whup his fat fuck ass," Eryk said.

Rory laughed as he fumbled for the other water bottle. "Have him do what I just did," he said. "Punishment enough."

A dense cloud slid over the sky, blocking out the sun for a moment, allowing Rory to stop squinting. Felt great, but he knew he was going to have to get back up and tackle the other two slabs. Maybe Erik would keep him in--,

Tink!

He glanced over to see Eryk moving rubble around with his foot. The sound of metal scraping against rock got Rory to his feet.

"The hell is that?"

"You tell me," Eryk said. "It's in there pretty good. Grab that hammer, give it a whack."

He grabbed the sledgehammer and walked over, balancing it underhand like a golf club. He moved chunks of concrete around to get a better look at what was making the sound.

"It's a box."

"I kinda' got that," Eryk said. "Hit it. Give it a good thunk."

"I don't want to break it."

"I kinda' do. Go ahead and hole-in-one that thing."

Rory smiled when he thought about launching a little metal box clean through a car window in the nearly empty parking lot. Instead he gave it an honest slap. The box dented in, came loose from the rubble and tumbled about six feet. Eryk let out a whoop and walked over to pick it up, while Rory let out a swear when he looked into the crater left by the box and a spotted something very different.

"Dude, you gotta check this out," Eryk said.

"No, dude, you gotta check *this* out, and I mean, like, now."

Eryk walked over with the cracked-open box in his hand. Rory lifted the sledgehammer to show Eryk a jawbone and part of a skull sticking out of the dirt.

"Oh sweet Jesus," Eryk said.

"Yeah. I wouldn't touch anything in that box until we get the cops here."

Eryk sighed. "Fuck, I can't afford that. Not tonight."

"It's probably a crime scene."

"Well, it's Friday night," Eryk said. "Rent night, and that's not a probably."

Rory and Eryk stood around the broken-up slab like they were grave robbers, which, at that point, they sort of were. Eryk fully opened the lid on the box and peeked in.

"So what the hell is in there, anyway?" Rory asked.

"A gun," Eryk said. "Thirty-eight Special, looks like. And a little leather-bound book, like what a bookie would keep."

"Dude, not cool. That gun probably killed our friend here."

Eryk closed the box and set it down before walking around the parking lot like he was working out a charley horse. Rory stared at the jawbone. He liked Eryk, but he wasn't fixin' to go to jail with him over someone neither of them knew. Eryk didn't even live in North Carolina when those slabs were first poured. Rory didn't know when that was, but he knew the difference between fresh-poured and the 'old 'n' weathered.'

Eryk walked back, wagging his finger in the air.

"Okay, check it out," he said. "We got to call the cops, I'm with you. I don't want to live with it on my conscience or have to look over my shoulder. But for real, I just got in here. We're not so flush we can skip a Friday night."

Eryk tapped on the box. Rory nudged chunks of concrete back in the cavity that birthed them.

"We leave this as rubble tonight, put a tarp over it. I'll make sure nobody stumbles into it, if I have to borrow traffic cones, whatever. I'll tell your boss I had to stop you from finishing; I'll make something up."

Rory pressed his palm into his forehead, pushing it up and over the bald spot, letting it slide down the back of his neck. If Samuel, now ten, hadn't told him to "fuck off" the last time they spoke, he might say he had too much to lose. But the reality was that he knew Eryk's hesitance was only partly to do with the bar.

"You want to read that little book, don't you?"

"Of course I do!" Eryk said. "Don't you?"

"I'm not as much a reader as you are. Hell, I barely read the books *you* write."

"Okay, then, don't you want me to tell you what's in the book?"

Rory laughed as he couldn't grab any solid objections. The murder could've happened fifty years ago. What's one more day?

"Alright, screw it," Rory said. "But I want cocktails, good ones. You tell me what it says, and we'll drink cocktails as a pact."

"Yeah, cocktails, okay."

Rory picked up the sledgehammer, set to go break up another one for good measure. Eryk grabbed his arm.

"Nah, man," Eryk said. "Let the cops dig them all up. If you still want to work, you can go get us a food run. And don't say shit to Lana. She'll make me put it back."

Yonder knew how to amp up a Friday night. The band had double-barrels of twang, and bluegrass wasn't even Rory's favorite music. But it was the place, a space that set everyone at ease, accepting the love out of anyone with something to say, giving gentle preference to anyone saying it through a 4 x 12 tube amp or a festival-christened PA. Rory had puttered around the bar all day, finding things to fix and not tell his boss about. Lana invited him to eat with them, and if she could feel the giddy secret the two had, she kept it to herself, assuming that it had to be less interesting than they thought it was. And Eryk kept to the office.

Around nine, Rory slid up to the bar. Eryk was tending, and of course it was busy, but Rory figured it was the last shot he had of learning what was in the book while he was still sober. Sober-ish.

"So what was it?" he asked when the band was hot and the bar cleared out a bit.

"A fucking speakeasy, dude."

"What, here?"

"Nope. Durham," Eryk said. "It was called the Park Club. Ritzy, based on what he wrote."

"Did he own it? Was it someone we'd heard about?"

Whoa, easy there." Eryk pulled a few bottles out from under the bottom shelf, from a spot that wasn't deserving of the name, "bottom shelf."

"Guy's name was Legs Diamond. A New York gangster. I think this was a branching-out thing for him. There's nothing on the web about him being in North Carolina. Mostly upstate New York."

"So, what, was it like his journal or something?"

Eryk chuckled. "Oh no, not so much," he said. "It's basically a hit list, I mean, that's part of it."

"A hit-list." Eryk made Rory a cocktail that didn't have a name, not that he knew of.

"Moonshiners, from what I could research. Like, every name in here, well, the ones that are crossed off – I looked them up, and they were killed."

"Okay, so what about our friend out there?"

"You got me," Eryk said. "There's still a few names I couldn't find."

"So that gun probably has a ton of bodies on it," Rory said.

"Oh, I figure."

"So that's it, a hit-list and a gun."

Eryk pulled the book out from behind the bar. He thumbed it opened and passed it over to Rory, who, even a little drunk, could tell what it was.

"Dude, this is a drink recipe."

"It's the cocktail you're drinking right now. You dig it?"

"Yeah, it's nice," Rory said. "So there's drink recipes in there too, then."

"A ton," Eryk said. "I scanned all those pages, so I have 'em."

They spent the night mixing cocktails, Eryk deciphering what amounted to a hundred-year-old handwriting, and Rory trying to clear his palate with a small handful of ice cubes between rounds.

"Who do you think buried it here?" Rory said.

"I have no idea," Eryk said. "But I'll tell you what; we'll find out pretty quick. It's gonna' be big news in a small town."

The night finished off with Rory and Eryk out back, standing in front of the rubble. Eryk didn't have the box; he figured he'd be more noticeable reburying it in the middle of the night than in the morning.

Rory tapped the sledgehammer's handle.

"Remind me to grab this tomorrow before the cops get here."

"Sure, sure," Eryk replied. They stared at the pit some more, swaying as the same damp air that boiled in the sun just clung in the moonlight. Eryk glanced at the sledgehammer.

"Hey," he said. "Just for shits, what do you think's under the other ones?"

THE
SALTY BANJO

Campari
Grapefruit
Bitters
Salted Rim

"I learned long ago, to never wrestle with a pig. You get dirty, and besides, the pig likes it"
— *George Bernard Shaw*

Amounts have been left out. Live a little.

PHILIP KIMBROUGH
THE PROPOSITION

To know my story is to know that you don't need to know much at all except to know that I am a salesman. My job is to understand what my client needs, solve those pains and make them feel like they are the most important person in the room. An exchange of goods for services rendered.

I'm a hooker with a company credit card.

After a whirlwind week of meetings, pitches, feedback and rejection over with, I sat at the hotel bar, contemplating canceling my last and final meeting of the night, when in walked Izzy.

Now, I had never really fantasized about it, but I guess, if I had to admit it, I always imagined that if I'd be propositioned for sex it would be like something out of a movie. A beautiful Julia Roberts type with long tan legs and a million-dollar smile sauntering up next to me, making idle chit chat while watching me play with the tan line where my wedding ring was supposed to be. She would say something like, "Care to buy me a drink," and I would happily have obliged.

She'd laugh at all of my stupid jokes, disarm me with her wit and make the idea of paying her for sex seem like a minute detail in an otherwise stellar random encounter. I'd take her up to the hotel room and she would take care of me, make me feel something, tug at my heart strings just enough to know that the next time I'd be in town that I'd be calling her up for her company.

Even prostitutes need repeat customers.

That's what I'd imagined.

I'd just finished my second vodka soda and was running my finger along the rim of the glass, deciding between ordering a single or double next, when she plopped down next to me. She smelled like she had taken a shit on the sidewalk, picked it up and used it as deodorant.

"You're lonely," she slurred. I couldn't tell if it was a question or a statement. She wasn't uneasy on the eyes, but the caked-on makeup didn't hide the scars and hard years she had lived like she probably hoped. She pulled a broken cigarette from the bowels of her bag, saw it dangling off the filter, huffed and threw it back in. "Bum one?"

"Excuse me?"

"Can I bum a fucking cigarette?".

"Sorry, don't smoke"

She let out a huff and closed her bag. "You buy me a drink and I'll take care of you." She went for the hard close.

My look of bewilderment must have told her I was slow on the pick up because she repeated herself.

"I'm Izzy. I'll take care of you if you buy me drink."

I looked around the bar, unsettled and unsure. Surely someone noticed that a prostitute had just plopped down at the table top and was on their way to escort her out.

Instead, the bartender stood on the opposite end, dry cloth and glass in hand, his attention solely focused on the basketball game playing on the television. Three associates behind the front desk were face down in their phones or helping other customers to check in. I turned back to Izzy. She stared through me, her eyes translucent, as if the drugs she was on had covered her eyes with frosted glass.

"I'm good. Thank you, though."

"Why're you by yourself then? Where's your ring at?"

It was a fair question to be sure and with the right person on the right night I'd me more than happy to share the story of why my ring was currently sitting in my right pants pocket; but not this person. Not this night.

"Sorry, but I think you have the wrong guy." I hopped up from my seat and walked to the other side of the bar. I hadn't sat back down before Izzy was up and beside me. I let out a contemptuous sigh, hoping she would get the message. My plate was more than full tonight and I couldn't afford to get distracted.

"You think you're better than me or something?"

"I don't." I motioned to the bartender for the check.

"You do, you think you're fucking better than me." She leaned closer. "Fucking news flash for you, Bro," she spat with venom. "You're not. You're just some fucking Joe, sitting in a hotel bar, with a tan line on your ring finger that stands out like a God Damn beacon yelling 'Someone fuck me.' And because you're in a suit all high and mighty, too chicken shit to ask for it yourself, you force people like me to engage you versus you coming up to me. Make me the be the lowlife. You think you're better than me."

"I really don't."

Her face was now next to mine, the heat of her breath against my ear and her stench camped out in my nostrils. I could feel my pants tighten against my better judgement. "You want one thing. You're no different than anyone else" Her hand sprang for my crotch and grabbed hold before I could process what was happening. She looked down at what she had grabbed hold to and smirked. "See."

I jumped up, knocking the barstool to the ground, my drink flying from my hand. I stumbled back. "What the fuck is wrong with you lady?"

She snarled a devilish smile, stood up and walked away.

A portly man waddled over as the bartender tossed me a towel to pat myself dry. The portly man introduced himself as Stephen, hotel security. He looked like he could barely keep his pantry secure, let alone a whole hotel. After I told him what happened, he let out a tsk tsk, turned to the front door where Izzy stood giddy. "Hey, you think you're being funny, do you?" He waved his fist in the air like an old Laurel and Hardy skit. "Do you want me to call the police, sir?"

"Police?" I froze. "No, that's okay."

"Are you sure?"

Police meant records. Police meant questions.

"I'm sure." Stephen eyed me. I flashed him a smile. "Really, I'm sure. I just feel bad I caused such a scene. Apologies. To you, too," I said to the bartender who gave me a nod.

Stephen let out his air and with it, a deep belly laugh. "It's not the first time that whore's been in here. I told her the next time I caught her in here, I'd have her ass hauled out in cuffs. Lucky day for her."

"Indeed."

"If she comes back in and bothers you anymore sir, you let me know, I'll take care of it immediately."

"Appreciate that. Thank you."

I bent down and lifted the stool back to the bar and took a seat. The bartender set another vodka soda in front of me and told me it was on the house. I raised it to him and took a long sip.

All eyes appeared to be on me now. Who could blame them? I

imagined the entire scene played out like the aftermath of a car crash - people couldn't help but look. I felt gross for her getting the best of me. I pulled the ring from my pocket and squeezed so hard I could feel my nails breaking skin. Izzy's equation had been fair. If I wasn't lonely, then why was I here.

It started with a simple text. After a long day of meetings, sitting in a similar bar in a similar hotel in a similar city, my phone had buzzed. *How're you doing?* She knew how I was doing, and she knew that I was alone. I was a couple of drinks in and with the truthfulness that liquid courage often provides I picked up the phone and texted her back.

Now, my phone lights up and dances on the bar top. A single text message. *I'm ready. 438.*

I slugged down the rest of my drink and stood. In the mirror behind the row of bottles, I could see it. I wasn't ready for what I was about to do. Didn't stop me from doing it though.

After the first few texts, role play felt like the logical next step. Nothing ever happened, but it was easy to pretend. If we just pretended, then we weren't really doing anything wrong. She started to join me on a couple of my trips. We got time together and it was a fun escape.

I handed the bartender my card to run and made my way to the elevator bay. Stephen gave me a wave. I just smiled politely back and pressed the arrow to head to the 4th floor.

It was in a similar elevator that she showed me the app to download to encrypt our messages. She had done some planning since our last role play. She knew that I'd be going to New York and thought what a better place to take it to the next level. Three thousand miles away it would be hard to feel guilty - or get caught. She had already booked us a hotel room

The elevator doors opened, and I stepped out into the hallway.

Turning right, I followed the signs down to room 438. The gray hallway was narrow, the stark white trim acting like the lights on a runway guiding me to my destination. As I approached the door, I felt the walls close in on me.

My lungs suddenly were unable to fill with air. My right arm shook, and I felt the cold sweat running down the side of my cheek. Before I lost my balance, I leaned back against the wall. It was all I could do not to spill my insides all over the gray ornate carpeting at my feet. Why was there so much grey?

I pulled out my phone, found her number and hit connect. She picked up on the third ring.

"Hi."

"What's wrong?"

I looked at the placard just beside my head. 438.

"I don't think I can go through with this."

The weight of the ring in my pocket became a boulder.

"Where are you," she asked.

"Right outside the room." I could hear her take a deep breath. How could she actually be on board with this? "What are we doing?" I asked.

"What needs to be done."

"No, this is isn't what needs to be done. We can figure something else out."

"Not that will make us this kind of money."

"I can't cheat on you."

"You're not. You're doing what needs to be done."

The phone buzzed in my hands and I pulled it away from my ear. I clicked open the message and staring back at me was a photo of me, my wife and our beautiful little girl. Most people just saw the breathing tube and colostomy bag. I saw a bright eyed, full of sun-shine 4-year-old.

Sometimes though, particularly after darker weeks at the hospital, all I saw were the hospital bills and drained bank accounts.

It started off as a joke. My wife asked what could help us make some quick cash to cover the latest round of prescriptions. I told her either lottery or selling my body. We both laughed.

A week later, I got the text asking how I was doing. They had both had a rough night at home and when I got to the house, I real-ized that she needed a night out. We wound up at Yonder and she pointed towards a cute girl sitting by herself and asked me how I'd go about picking her up if she wasn't there. I laughed and she asked me again.

I told her I wouldn't pick her up.

"You wouldn't?"

"No, I'd sell her." Find the pain, solve the problem.

Six months later, about five different role plays and test runs over with, here I was standing in a hotel, about to knock on the door of a client my wife had handpicked to pay me $500 bucks to sleep with for an hour.

I heard my wife call my name and I pulled the phone back.

"You can do this. We love you so much."

I hung up the phone, wiped my brow and took a deep breath. Time to sell.

I faced the door, knocked three times as discussed, put my hands in pockets and waited.

The ring danced around my fingers.

The doorknob turned.

I told myself the sacrifice would be worth it.

I doubted the ring would ever fit properly again.

CAROLINA BACKROADS

Moonshine
Mint
Watermelon
Lime

"Anything that comes out of the South is going to be called grotesque by the northern reader, unless it is grotesque, in which case it's going to be called realistic."
– Flannery O'Connor

Amounts have been left out. Live a little.

STACIE LEININGER
LLAMA JUICE

"It's about time Bob Dinkerman got shanked." I crossed my arms over my chest and added, "Sad it happened behind Yonder. Bad for business." I paused to pull the collar of my button up shirt. Damn thing was digging into my neck, "His murder came a couple years too late..."

"Objection!" I got cut off by some overpriced suit wearing young Defense Attorney; I guess she wanted to use this case to make a name for herself. Epic fail if you ask me.

"What?" I snapped back. "How can you object to the truth?"

I shook my head and adjusted myself in the creaking wooden chair abandoned in storage in the 1960's. A few months prior to trial, the courthouse got flooded; it was entertaining watching these suits scramble to locate viable furniture. National news stations flashed images of industrial fans blowing into empty rooms. A lot of good that did, my nose was offended by a lingering scent of mold mixed with the Judge's Old Spice and halitosis. I refrained from offering him a breath mint as I leaned forward.

A half circle of vulturistic news reporters buzzed in mismatched Church pews. Hard wood pressed against my ass, bringing me back to my Catholic School years. My eyes rested on man in front dressed all in black. I half waited for him to hold up a wafer and proclaim, "The Body of Christ."

Numbness tickled my left butt cheek; I shook my leg to wake it up. Now, I was certain Sister Mary Robertson would waddle in wielding her metal ruler and scream at me for slouching. The thought of her navy-blue habit snapped me back to a perfectly erect posture. Instinctively I gave a sign of the Cross and said a quick "Hail Mary" under my breath, just for safe measures. She had been dead for over a decade; but I wasn't chancing it.

The judge clapped his gavel down. Several news reporters jumped. As for me, I peered up at Judge McAurthor's stern weather worn wrinkled face and held back my contempt while he stated, "For the last time, stick to the facts!"

"I fail to see how that is not a fact. His deplorable actions should've gotten him killed years back. We all know that." I stated in a matter-of-fact tone. Luck would have it the Defense Attorney requested I be treated as a hostile witness.

Judge McAurthor waved his gavel at the prosecution and requested they remind me I was under oath; followed by, "It's important your witness stick to the facts."

Palm raised, the prosecutor motioned for silence while all those legal assholes discussed me. Metal detectors had alerted the cops at the entrance of my flask; how I yearned for a swig of anything 80 proof or higher. Finally, after several banter filled minutes, I was allowed to continue with my re-telling of the events leading up to Bob's death.

It was after hours when I lugged a white plastic garbage bag to the dumpster where I found the deceased in a pool of his own blood. Our county had her first murder of the year and it happened behind Yonder Southern Cocktails & Brew. If anyone deserved a death like this it was this damn asshole too, if you ask me; then again, no one asks me anything. It's not like I really matter. I only clean shit.

A person can only stomach a certain amount of dried vomit and bubble-gum under tables. But I digress. Most people glance over the half-filled bottles of colorful liquid lined up behind the bar, across the wooden shelf running along a red brick wall and forget there's a human who makes it all pretty. Dust be damned; I clean it all!

My dingy grey mop methodically wipes away all evidence of humans from the Velcro-like floors. When we're done, you can eat off that wood; except there are laws preventing such behavior. Then, there are my rags; they remove spider webs and dust from paintings hung on the walls. Ambiance and cleanliness are as important as good food and drinks; just ask those guys who assess eating establishments. Thankfully, Bob's blood was taken care of by a crime scene clean up crew; I do hate cleaning up blood.

It all began a couple weeks before that day, when a nice woman from an upstate New York, a place called Troy, stopped in on her vacation. She's a tattooed red head standing all of five-feet-four and carries herself as if she were twice that size. Her light pink shoulder bag read "Prada" while her t-shirt and jeans screamed second-hand shop at best. The ginger weight of her walk made her cork board heals soundless; a viper in disguise.

I watched her blaze through the doors before we were open for daily business and grab a seat at the bar like she owned the joint. With her, came a strong odor of roses gagging me where I stood. She yelled at Eryk, the new co-owner and bartender, "Yo ho ho! Rumor has it you bought up part of this establishment." She knocked on the bar and added, "I figured since I was in the area I'd stop in."

"Kathy!" Eryk chuckled and poured a beer. "You're the last person I'd expect to see here," he said with a mischievous grin.

She snatched up the drink, chugged it halfway down, and slapped a twenty down next to it. Her voice filled the empty room, "You know, the hardcore scene is a little dull since Jimmy got screwed by Tessa. Then there was the fraud issue with Tiny and Bulldog."

Eryk laughed, "Can you go anywhere without bringing the whole team with you?"

Kathy held up her glass and responded, "Where's the fun in that? Besides, I'm here on vacation. And who else will fill you in on the juicy gossip?"

"Facebook," Eryk replied. "Or did you forget?"

"Nah," she said and finished her beer, "Good ale, by-the-by." She clanked the empty glass on the bar pushing the bill towards Eryk.

I watched the foam slink down the glass and wondered how soon she'd leave. No such luck. The two continued to converse while I cleaned. This woman complained about how quiet our area was and had the audacity to say we needed screaming edgy music. Apparently, where she's from angry music guides a faster pace lifestyle overlooking the Hudson River. One bit I appreciated; she complimented our area on our friendliness; people hold doors for one another here a courtesy on the verge of extinction in upstate New York.

Before we knew it, staff and regulars had poured in. Appetizers filled trays carried by smiling waitresses. Several plastic pitchers passed by me some empty while others carried liquid. To the amusement of a growing crowd, Eryk tossed a bottle in the air. Sangria returned to his outstretched hand to the delight of those around him. Drinks slid across a well polished bar top while music played through speakers hidden above.

Tucked in a corner, Kathy danced to a different beat. I assumed her iPhone was playing that hardcore crap she raved about. For once, I was thankful for a clogged toilet; I tucked myself into the men's room to fix the issue. When I returned, Bob lay flat.

Lance, a Polish immigrant who learned English from New York City subway graffiti and newspapers yelled, "Dead man!"

Kathy held up her glassful of beer and calmly stated, "Nah, he'll wake up soon." Then proclaimed, "Not a drop spilled!"

Several patrons cheered her on while Eryk shook his head. In a single moment, our reputation crumbled like a sand sculpture under a giant wave; Bob had grabbed her ass for which he got cold clocked.

"Her next beer's on me!" a male voice called out. I glanced his way to see James Closterfelt holding up a bill. Today's outfit consisted of electric blue pants and a pink shirt.

An unfamiliar female tenor voice shouted, "I'll get her a pitcher!"

In a matter of minutes State Police were busying gathering statements. One asked me what I had seen of the incident. I recapped events leading up to it then explained what I removed from the clogged toilet. Apparently, these Troopers don't have the constitutions for my line of work, this guy's face turned green before he walked away.

Off to the side, Kathy nursed another drink while she waved at the unconscious Bob Dinkerman being loaded onto a gurney. Several patrons cheered while he was taken away via ambulance. Meanwhile, I was forced to clean up the blood his nose left behind.

Days passed without further issues. I assumed Bob was still hospitalized when rumors hit my ears. Multiple bars raved about Kathy's heroic acts; one story had her doing a roundhouse kick breaking his jaw while another claim involved her handbag. Several bars and local stores had banned Bob from their premises, forcing him to travel two counties over for his drinks and underwear shopping.

Just like any good story, upon circulation, other incidents involving the aforementioned miscreant surfaced and new ones were created. It didn't take long for law enforcement to take further actions. I wish I could have been at his place for that search warrant delivery. The look on his mother's face must have been priceless! She may have been on oxygen and in a wheelchair, but that woman was just as mean as Sister Mary Robertson. I wouldn't put it past her to have a hidden ruler in that chair; one time, she ran over my foot and laughed. Laughed I tell you!

During the investigation news media let everyone know that Police found a greenhouse in their backyard, filled with marijuana plants and few bricks of cocaine. My favorite was the USB drive, on which were pictures of him using elephants to plow a cotton field and videos of him having sex in a churchyard. I'm still perplexed as to where those elephants came from and who would fuck that man let alone in a churchyard.

Other felonies included over $2,000 worth of restaurant grease "allegedly" stolen from local establishments, a felony as of 2012. Apparently, he was attempting to turn his truck into a grease reliant vehicle. Poor bastard. At lease we now know why he frequented the junkyard for Ford Ranger parts. We all can rest easy knowing he experimented on a Ford instead of a Chevy.

It was when the Police found the llamas tied up in a far corner of his yard they called for a full scale search. Why he had llamas is still a mystery. To think, this all started because he grabbed a stranger's ass; wish she had arrived sooner, we could've gotten rid of this son-of-a-bitch sooner. Good riddance Bob!

After his disappearance, I began eavesdropping on conversations while I cleaned. I found out the woman he sexually assaulted had started a "Track the Bob" website. Believe me, I went straight to her page and read the stories. People came out of the woods to tell their own versions of what they witnessed, and I assure you there was no drunken clown juggling stuffed animal poodles. Others recanted stories of past experiences and then there were Bob sightings all over our country. One person placed him in Salt Lake City Utah. While another showed a video of a man up a tree, in the state of Virginia, screaming at a barking Doberman Pinscher, "I'm not him!"

Two whole weeks passed before I walked out to find Bob sprawled eagle in a pool of his own blood. For a brief moment, I contemplated tossing him into the dumpster and allowing the sanitation department to finish the cleanup. But, as I previously stated, I can't stand blood.

Even though the crime scene clean-up crew sterilized the area to a point where one could, in theory, eat off the ground I still cringed at the mere thought of setting foot in that space. Eyes closed, I see Bob floating in a crimson pool next to a blue dumpster tagged by a teenager who couldn't spell "fuck." Who puts an "h" in "fuck" anyways? His parents must be proud of those fifteen minutes of fame; then again, maybe not.

It didn't take long for the Police to narrow their search down. Personally, I was shocked to hear Bob's own mother was a suspect. As far as I knew she wasn't able to walk; that's why he lived there, to help her out. The shit hit the fan when an arrest warrant was issued on separate charges and come to find out the drugs were hers. That bitch was faking it all these years! The wheelchair was a ploy! That spry 72-year-old woman knew karate. I wouldn't have believed it if I hadn't seen it myself!

A construction crew sat at the bar eating lunch when Mrs. Dinkerman rolled by their tool-laden parked truck. That woman ripped off her oxygen and did a roundhouse kick to a young Deputy and spun to run. We watched through the big front window as she got nailed by a shovel. Once she crumbled to the ground Kathy set the shovel back on the truck. Turns out, she took a weekend trip out here to see about the commotion for herself. She had just walked up to Yonder when she saw Mrs. Dinkerman attack the Deputy; so, she helped.

Needless-to-say, I never thought I'd be a witness in court; but there I was giving testimony. Once everything was done, Mrs. Dinkerman was found guilty of multiple charges and will serve a life sentence. As for Kathy, her actions were ruled self defense; clearing her of all charges. And in case you are wondering what happened to the llamas, they were shipped off to a petting zoo and now have a drink named after them.

THE EL RAY

Mescal
Carrot
Pineapple
Habanero

"I ain't saying you're a liar, because that wouldn't be polite. But I'll tell you this, ma'am: If I loved liars, I'd hug you to death."
– Jim Thompson (Pop 1280)

Amounts have been left out. Live a little.

GREG HERREN
MOIST MONEY

The United States military trained my father to be a ruthless killing machine in Vietnam, then turned him loose on his hometown of Leicester, North Carolina.

Me? Yeah, no fucking thanks. Dad was enough military for me, thank you very much—waking me up every morning at 6 a.m., inspecting my room and testing the tightness of the made bed with a quarter. He was a drunk by then, and a mean one…but he was always up at six, always smelling like last night's liquor, cigarettes and whore.

I'm paying for college by taking my clothes off for money. A male stripper—a go-go boy, if you prefer. It means I watch what I eat, spend a minimum of an hour in the gym almost every day, and get to write off bikinis, underwear, jockstraps, and thongs as business expenses.

It's a fucking living, okay?

My preference is booking gay bars. I like gay bars. Gay men are friendlier, nicer, and tip better. I make bank when I dance in a gay bar, and it doesn't really require a whole lot of work. Eye contact, some minor flirting, the occasional touch here and there—always good for a couple of bucks. The older ones are a lot more handsy than the younger ones, but they also have more cash in their wallets.

Bachelorette parties, like the one we're doing tonight, are the fucking worst.

The *worst.*

You'd think women would be a lot easier to entertain than gay men, but when you get a bunch of them together without their men, liberally dose them with serious tequila shots and expensive fruit colored drinks with umbrellas and cherries, and they turn into a pack of ravening wolves. They do things they'd never let their man suspect they'd do. They like to touch dicks, like to see if they can get you hard, like to see how big you get when you get hard, and then give you a couple of ones for getting groped like a cheap whore in a dive bar full of sailors. They like to jump on you and wrap their legs around your waist while deep tongue kissing you with their breath smelling like cigarettes and sour liquor and breath mints. They want you to perform for them like a wind-up monkey and the money is never, ever, even close to what you can make in a good crowded gay bar. I work in a gay bar in Atlanta or New Orleans or DC? Wads of sweaty cash shoved into whatever I'm wearing and into my socks and boots, moist money to flatten out and count and pay the bills after making that deposit on Monday morning.

Moist money spends like every other kind.

Bachelorette parties? The flat fee for the night—an hour—is $250, and if I'm lucky and they're particularly drunk, I might pick up another hundred in tips. And the whole time I'm fucking hustling, thrusting my hips and dancing like I'm humping one of them, pelvic thrust after pelvic thrust and moving my hips around in a circle, all while someone is grabbing my ass or tweaking my nipples or groping my dick.

At least gay men know to pay extra for that, you know?

I was supposed to be off this weekend. I'd told Clarice at the agency I wanted this weekend off to work on my final paper for my goddamned Anthropology class. I didn't have a paper due—I'd just worked every weekend for several months and my roommate was going out of town and I just wanted to spend the whole weekend by myself in my apartment, walking around naked and doing whatever the hell I pleased. But one of the other guys got food poisoning and I was bored so I said sure, which is why I am in this car heading for a yokel bar called Yonder, of all things, to entertain some horny women who've drank too much and want to act all wild and crazy before going home and passing out in bed with their men, whom they haven't fucked in over a week.

Yeah, fun.

Yonder. Who fucking names their bar *that?*

Some hillbilly redneck yokel, that's who. Probably best to keep my sexuality on the down-low anyway. Stupid straight women don't like to know the muscular body they're groping would rather be touched by a man, anyway.

Bachelorette parties also call for *gimmicks.* The cop is a popular one, with the tight uniform that can be ripped off in one fluid motion, and of course, the goddamned trick handcuffs. The stupid bitches like to play like they *like* being handcuffed, that it's proof of how sexually adventurous they are, as their friends all make that high-pitched squealing *ooooh* sound which is probably the sound they fake with their men while they're getting fucked.

These women have rented the bar out on this night for their party, which means they have cash.

Which *sort of* makes getting groped by a bunch of straight women and pretending I like it worth my while, I suppose. I need to get whatever moist money I can coax out of these bitches. You can bet I'm gonna have a big grin on my face and put on a good show for them.

The thing that sucks about the cop uniforms is that it's against the law to impersonate a police officer. Which means we can't get dressed until we're actually there—a couple of the guys a couple years back put on the outfits before they went to the party and got pulled over for a busted tail light and then got run in by a hard-ass little-dicked deputy with something to prove.

Guys with little dicks always have something to prove.

So, we're going to slip into the bar through the back alley—Ty, who's driving, worked everything out with the bar owner—and get dressed in the back office, and then we're going to slip back out and come in through the front door.

God how I hate the stupid cop routine. Ty is good at it, so I'm letting him take the lead. I'll just stand back and slap my nightstick into my palm while he warns them about disturbing the peace—and when he says *I don't know, ladies, just what we're going to do with you* that's my cue to toss the nightstick aside and rip open my shirt.

Seriously, it's so much easier to dance in gay bars rather than do this stupid routine.

And now we're pulling up behind the bar, and Ty is grinning his stupid grin at me. He's straight and gets off on how women eat up his body—he doesn't mind the worship of gay men, but at least with a female audience he might get laid—and I wonder for a moment if he ever got that gonorrhea infection cleared up.

Not my problem.

I grab my bag. He knocks on the back door—*tap tap tap*— which opens and a young woman waves us in. She's not bad, if you like the type—all tits and hips and a little waist and big hair that probably could brush against the bottom of a cloud—and she hustles us into the office. She closes the door behind us and looks up and down like she's deciding which one of us gets the pleasure of her company later.

All yours, Ty.

"All right," she says, her accent thick and honey-drenched, her white teeth slightly crooked in the front, which makes her upper lip pouty. She's looking at Ty, who's taking off his sweatpants. All he has on underneath is a bright yellow thong, that looks even brighter and more yellow against his dark tanning salon tan.

Definitely all his—the hook was in her mouth and all he has to do was reel her in. She won't fight the line.

"All right," she says again, tearing her eyes off the bulge in his thong. "They're playing *pin the cock on the hunk* right now. Once they finish, I'm going to give them a round of tequila shots. Your cue to knock on the front door is when I blink the lights out front. Then you pound on the door, and I'll answer."

I'm already snapping my pants closed and slipping my feet into the black patent-leather cop shoes. Let's just get this over with, already. I want to get back home away from this bullshit as soon as I can, smoke a joint and chill.

"The bachelorette's name is Kaylee," she says, pausing at the door to give Ty's ass a look as he bends over to fasten his shoes. "Her fiancee's name is Brandon, if you want to like bring it up or anything."

I freeze as the door shut behinds her.

Kaylee? Brandon?

The names have to be a coincidence.

But what are the odds?

Granted, it seems everyone these days is named Kaylee or Kayla or McKayla or some variation of that, and Brandons are as common as Mikes used to be...so it had to be a coincidence.

It couldn't possibly be Kaylee Lawless and Brandon Perry, could it?

Ty is talking to me with a big grin on his face, but I don't hear a word he's saying. My heart is pounding so loudly in my ears I couldn't hear anything at the moment.

Kaylee Lawless. Brandon Perry.

I'd dreamed of killing them both so many times, so many nights when I was living in that goddamned dorm at juvie. Slitting them both from ear to ear with a particularly sharp blade, using a machete to separate their heads from their necks, making Kaylee take a gun barrel into her mouth like she was sucking a dick and pulling the trigger while he watched, helpless, unable to do anything as I blew her brains out. I dreamed of breaking every one of his fingers and toes, slowly and carefully, making sure to break them in a way so they wouldn't heal right. I thought about rigging their cars to explode with them inside. I prayed for their deaths, my hate for the two of them slowly shifting from blazing hot to implacable, cold, determined, dispassionate.

"Anger is why everyone winds up here," I remember one of the counselors telling me.

If the bachelorette was, indeed, Kaylee Lawless…I'd have to remember to stay cool.

The odds were against it, I thought again as Ty and I walked around to the front of the building in our cop outfits, hoping no patrol car came by. We stood by the front door of the bar, waiting for the lights to flicker, listening to the screeching cackling of the party inside, Ty's grin getting wider and wider and wider.

The lights flicker.

Ty pounds on the door. "OPEN UP! POLICE!" He shouts, his voice deepening, taking on the resonance of authority. There's quiet inside now, and the door opens, and Big Boobed Heaven Hair stands there, looking worried, and says something, but I can't hear her because my heart is pounding loudly again because I can see past her, can see the bitches of the bachelorette party, and it's her, all right, I'd recognize her anywhere, she's older but still has that same cat-shaped face with the aloe-eyes flickering green beneath long lashes, and I recognize some of the other girls, too.

It's like it's meant to be, like God wants me to do this.

I haven't seen her in almost ten years. Ten years ago, when she and her shit-for-brains boyfriend made my life a living hell in good ole Leicester, North Carolina, calling me fag, making fun of my clothes, mocking me. Kaylee and Brandon, Brandon and Kaylee, the richest kids in town, the two who were meant to be King and Queen of everything, the ones whose lead everyone else followed.

Which meant making sure I had no friends, that no one had my back, and they could do whatever the fuck they wanted to me.

Brandon and his fucking buddies on the football team. Kaylee's face, her eyes lit up with cruel excitement, as they held me down and stripped my clothes off me, me screaming and begging to be let go, turning me over and Kaylee handing them the broom—

Nothing happened to them, of course, boys will be boys and all that, and their parents pretty much owned the cops and everything in Leicester.

Maybe I shouldn't have stolen Brandon's new car and poured gasoline on the seats and tossed a match in it. Maybe I shouldn't have pissed into the carpet in Kaylee's car.

Then I wouldn't have gone to juvie and straightened my life out.

But who knows what might have happened if the Leicester cops had done their jobs and arrested the sick fucks for raping me with a broom?

The women look solemn—except for one, the one who hired us and made the arrangements, she's smirking—and then Ty does it, he yells whatever it is he always yells and is ripping off his shirt and his pants and I automatically do the same, looking at the faces of the women, wondering if I know any of them, wondering if any of them recognize me.

I was fourteen when I was sentenced and sent away.

I doubt they ever gave me another thought.

And I'm whipping off my shirt and pants, tossing them onto an empty table, standing there with my cop cap and my sunglasses on still, just my boots and socks and a day-glo green thong, and I turn around and twerk my fine ass for them.

I learned to twerk in juvie.

They're all whooping it up now, yelling and screaming and shrieking as Ty and I bump and grind our way through them, dollar bills being shoved into our thongs as we work it, and I can feel my dick getting a bit hard because I'm thinking about how easy it would be to kill this bitch right here and now, put my hands around her throat and squeeze until her eyes pop and her face turns purple and she gurgles.

And it comes to me, how I can do it and get away with it.

How humiliating for Brandon to have his one-and-only, his true love, die while having a stripper grind his dick on her.

You just, I learned in juvie, have to make it look like an accident.

My father taught me how to kill when I was a boy, I remember as I bounce my dick at some redhead who squeals and pinches my nipples. I lick my lips back at her as I remember Dad telling me how easy it is to slip a needle or a screwdriver into the ear and brain. How to close a windpipe. How to twist someone's head with the right amount of force so the neck snaps.

I can do this.

I just need the chance.

The music changes and I'm sweating, which is fine—people always like sweaty muscles—and mine are defined, thick, beautiful, from hours in the juvie gym and all the time I've spent in the gym since then. My abs ripple when I roll them and get a twenty from an older woman who looks like she's seen and done it all, and I kiss her heavily made up cheek.

It's inevitable, isn't it?

Bachelorette parties always want the strippers to do a show for the bachelorette, grind on her and get her to lick biceps and nipples and things, do things her fiancée would be mortified to see her do.

I just have to wait and make money until the time is ripe.

About four songs later, the older woman drags a chair out to the middle of the floor and beckons Kaylee over.

Kaylee isn't the same girl she was fourteen years ago, tiny and compact and her waist so small I could wrap my arm around her twice. Her eyes have hardened with time, and she's put on some weight around the middle, and her ass has spread out a bit too. But that spark of mean is still in her slanted green eyes, and I know if she's ever given me a second thought since that night with the broom, it's to remember how hard it was getting the smell of my piss out of her car.

Bitch.

Ty's going to town on her now, one leg up over her shoulder and swinging his crotch in front of her face, with all the other women making lewd noises and comments, and then I move in for the tag team, the double-dicking, as Ty calls it.

She smiles up at me as I put my leg up over the opposite shoulder from Ty's and we both bump and grind our groins into her face. Ty moves away, and I lean down and whisper in her ear, "You and Brandon should have killed me when you had the chance," and I have the exquisite pleasure of seeing the look on her face when she recognizes me, realizes who I am—

--and before she can say anything, I shift my weight so the chair falls over backward, bringing me with it.

I twist her head quickly before we hit the floor and hear her neck snap.

I let my own head hit the floor and fall to the side, groaning.

"Kaylee?" I hear someone say as I try to get to my feet.

And then someone starts to scream.

Ty is down on the floor, checking her out. He was pre-med before he dropped out of Duke. "Somebody call an ambulance!" he shouts.

I collapse back to the floor, burying my face in my hands so they can't see me smile, I can't help it.

Brandon, I'm coming for you next.

YONDER
OLD FASHIONED

Bourbon
Ginger Syrup
Orange
Cherry
Angostura

"My own experience has been that the tools I need for my trade are paper, tobacco, food, and a little whiskey."
– William Faulkner

Amounts have been left out. Live a little.

BRUCE ROBERT COFFIN
OLD FASHIONED

B elle sat in her usual place at the end of the bar, seemingly oblivious to the boisterous Saturday night crowd. A classy lady both in dress and the graceful way she carried herself. There was nothing pretentious about her. I scurried down to the other end of the counter to take care of a thirsty-looking foursome that had wandered in, but my thoughts remained with the raven-haired beauty.

I am the proprietor of Yonder Southern Cocktails and Brew. Yonder has only been about six months, but I think I'm beginning to get the hang of this business. The bank loan officer tells me that it'll take a year or more before I begin to turn a profit. Bars and restaurant are "high risk" he says. I figure he's dead wrong. Hell, the thirsty crowd I hang with should put me in the black, and keep me there.

I had been searching for the perfect locale to open Yonder when I stumbled upon this place. Located right smack dab in the middle of Hillsborough on West King, the district was once a manufacturing hub for North Carolina. Brick and mortar storefronts, repurposed into coffee shops, restaurants, and clothing boutiques, lined the gentrified neighborhood. There's even a radio station. As I perused the area, I knew the one thing the neighborhood was missing was a classy watering hole. And 114 West King had the most important feature on my wish list, the lease was cheap, at least compared to most of the other places I'd looked. But beyond price, the space possessed a distinct southern charm. Its decorative high tin tray ceiling with rounded edges, walls of exposed brick, massive wooden beams, and distressed hardwood flooring all spoke to me. I hurried into the realtor's office and signed the one year lease an hour later. No dickering. No haggling. No clue.

It was a busy night, but then Saturdays usually are. Between filling table orders for the waitstaff and struggling to keep up with thirsty bar patrons, I barely managed a glance at Belle. I had dubbed her with that moniker, before knowing her actual name, because it just seemed to fit. In truth, I don't know a lot about her. The only words she's ever uttered to me are, "old fashioned" and "thank you". Just four words, but they flowed off Belle's tongue as sweetly as drop of blackstrap molasses. I catch another glimpse as she sips daintily from the rim of her glass. She never speaks to anyone but me, likewise my other customers pay her no mind. Some folks just want to be left alone.

As far as drinks go, I whip up a pretty decent old fashioned. But for Belle I always go the extra mile, using only top shelf whiskey, two dashes of bitters, and my own syrup concoction, topped with a fresh orange slice. I figure a classy lady like that would prefer the real deal to some fruity imitation millennial drink.

Hanging high above the liquor shelves on the wall behind the bar is a large antique mirror. The three arched glass panels encased in an ornamental scalloped edged metal frame, backlit by a strand of lights on a dimmer, really draw the eye. The local second hand dealer soaked me good on the price, but I figured what the hell, it would be Yonder's centerpiece after all. The antiquarian couldn't tell me much about the mirror's history, only to say that the craftsman who'd created the piece was hanged for murder. After he'd imparted that little nugget, I'd have paid anything he asked. With all the renovation work that followed, I'd nearly forgotten about the mirror until a month or so after I'd officially opened for business. As soon as the mirror went up, so did my profits. Belle appeared shortly thereafter.

Yonder gets its name from that word the locals always toss around when giving directions. Not that pretentious light breaking through yonder window bullshit, more like that southern "it's over yonder a ways". The other reason for the name was that the Y easily transformed into a martini glass. Great imagery for the lighted sign hanging out front.

We get all types in here. The yuppie college crowd, blue collar lite beer drinkers, martini drinkers, obviously, and the hard drinking middle-aged type. Occasionally, we do get the type that wants to fight after a couple of drinks. Thankfully, there's always an off duty cop or fire fighter ready to extinguish the threat. Far cheaper for me to comp a few rounds than shell out for a bouncer.

I steal another look at Belle and she gifts me with a smile and a subtle nod, her signal that she wants a refill. I grab a clean glass and get right to the task. Belle always has two drinks during her visits. No more, no less. And she never orders food. I guess the lady just wants what she wants. Who am I to argue a woman who knows her own mind? Smoothly I set a fresh drink and napkin in front of her and remove the empty. My heart flutters as she gifts me with another smile. My Belle.

One of my regulars, seated at a four top, makes eye contact and holds up four fingers, indicating another round. I give him a thumbs up and signal one of my waitstaff to get after it.

I've become fascinated with the history of Hillsborough, specifically the story of Edwin Hopper, the artist responsible for Yonder's intricate mirror. By all accounts, Hopper was a conundrum, married, talented artist, father of five, and serial philanderer. He was tried and convicted for murdering one of the women with whom he had had an affair. The victim had been stabbed to death in her bed. Fifty-three stab wounds to be exact. I'd always wondered who was tasked with counting them. And really, what difference did the number of wounds make anyway? Dead was dead, right?

According to the newspaper reports in the library archives, Hopper was found in possession of the murder weapon. He went to his grave professing his innocence. Not an unusual occurrence, most convicts never admit their guilt, even when caught red-handed, but it certainly makes things more interesting if true. What if Hopper was innocent? Who would have wanted to set him up for murder? My first thought was Hopper's wife, Eunice. Maybe she tired of Mr. H's philandering and killed two birds with one stone. Literally.

I grabbed two empty glasses from a tray atop the bar and plunged them into the hot soapy water, gave them a quick once over with a sponge, rinsed, then set them aside to dry. As I repeated the process, I watched the mindless conversation between a slightly intoxicated young man and an equally youthful woman seated at the bar. She was drinking club soda and appeared to be bored to tears. Some things never change. As I looked at the two of them I couldn't help but wonder what she was thinking. Was she really bored or simply hiding behind a mask of boredom? Perhaps she was secretly planning the drunk raconteur's demise.

I stole another glance down the bar toward Belle, hoping that she might need something from me. She was staring as if transfixed at the mirror above the bar. I wondered if she was as taken with the antique as I was, or if there was another reason for her interest.

It wasn't until my third trip to the library that I uncovered information concerning the victim in the Hopper case. The librarian who had helped me locate information within the digital archives, had been doing some additional sleuthing on my behalf. She led me to the building's musty basement where sagging cardboard boxes stood stacked atop wooden pallets. I followed her to a far corner where a banker's lamp sat on a wooden table. Also on the table lay a dusty green file folder. After confessing her growing fascination with the Hopper case, the librarian left me to my own devices and I dug into the new information. The stabbing victim's name was Libby Crabtree. According to the article, Ms. Crabtree was a transplant from the city of New York, having come to the Carolina's for work. Despite the fact the headline indicated that the story was about the victim, the reporter kept switching gears and writing about the Hoppers. I guess the heinous nature of the crime, Hopper's fame, and his tawdry affair with the victim, were simply too juicy to avoid. I had nearly made it to the bottom of the folder's mildew-covered contents when I saw something that stopped me in my tracks. The article contained two grainy black and white photographs. The first was a picture of Ms. Libby Crabtree. I recognized the face instantly. Fifty years may have passed since the murder was committed, but the last time I saw her, she looked exactly the same. I leaned in for a closer look at the second photo. It was an overall of the crime scene. Mounted on the wall directly above the bed was the very same mirror that now hung behind my bar at Yonder's. Hopper had created the antique mirror for his lover. I sat back in my chair, staring at the two photos. I realized that whatever had happened in that bedroom, the mirror had seen it all. Libby Crabtree's mirror.

At closing time, I began removing glasses from the bar. The waitstaff followed suit at each table. As with every watering hole, once the flow of liquor is cutoff people flood toward the exit. I was ushering the last of the stragglers out the front door when a middle-aged woman stopped and turned to face me.

"Do you mind if I ask you a question?" she asked. Her accent betrayed her as a northerner, her excitement was obvious.

I knew what was coming, of course, but I played along. "Not at all," I said.

"Is it true what my friends told me?"

"Is what true?" I asked.

She pointed toward the end of the bar. "The drink you always leave there on the bar. Is that really for a ghost?"

I turned my head to where Belle had been seated only a moment before, but the stool was empty. A glass containing an untouched old fashioned sat atop the bar. I turned back to the woman and smiled. "Don't tell me you believe in ghosts."

THE HARRIKIN

Tennessee Whisky
Passionfruit
Lime
Cherry

"She was a page torn from a calendar, a year folded neatly and laid aside in some place you never look."
– William Gay (TWILIGHT)

Amounts have been left out. Live a little.

RENATO BRATKOVIČ
THE BIG SPLASH

If someone had ever told me I was going to die underwater, I'd probably have died from laughter. Drown in whiskey? Yeah, maybe. But in the water? A swimmer like me? Hahahaha!

Anyway, I barely have enough time to breathe in. Strong hands belonging to one of Fat Phil's gorillas plunge my head into the water. I have to learn not to fuck with Fat Phil the hard way I guess. Well, at least I'm going to die clean, ha ha…

A classic scene from a movie. An interrogatee, a good cop and a bad cop. Me, my former schoolmate and a guy I had never been unlucky enough to meet until now.

For more than two hours I've been staring at their moving lips, clenched teeth and spraying foam — and pieces of the burger the good one is stuffing into his mouth.

"Look," the good one says. "I only want what's best for you, my friend. You're okay as far as I know you, but if you don't spit out what we want to hear, we…"

As far as he knows me. Fucking loser no one liked — not his schoolmates, professors neither. Hell, even his parents hated him. I admit I had a beer with him a couple of times if he was buying. But my friend? Let's not exaggerate, okay?

"Listen, 'friend,'" I say and lean on my elbows. "When I have something for you, I'll be happy to come around, but now if that's it I'd say it's time to say goodbye?" The good one nods and the bad one bangs his fist against the table: "We're not done with you yet, pal!"

"Listen, if this guy," — I point my finger at the good cop — "dares to call me his friend, that doesn't mean that you and me are more than just two unlucky individuals breathing the same air in the same stinking interrogation room due to some evil twist of fate — we're not even a "p" in pal! Bye!"

"Hey," my schoolmate says. "If you have anything, just call me, okay?"

When I'm out, I breathe a sigh of relief.

At first, you feel anxiety — you're aware there's a whole bunch of air around you that you don't have access to. You start feeling muscle cramps and feel a panic attack coming on, you shake your head and let the last bubbles of air and muffled noises through your teeth. But your hands are tied behind your back and hands of a man twice your size are holding you in a position you can never escape.

After a couple of steps, a car stops next to me. The car I know. A co-driver's window opens.

"Get in!"

I melt into the backseat and we screech in the direction I know very well — the Fat Phil estate.

Back in his best days, Phil was a champion in martial arts I can't even spell or pronounce. A promising young guy, who went down the evil road. He started offering protection to bar owners and later added illegal substance delivery to his offer. His business grew quickly (as well as his belly — that's why the fighting side of his business is executed by two apes in this car.) His regular client base consisted of businessmen, artists, politicians and similar kind of vermin, who address themselves as "the elite". That's why they still haven't stepped on his toes.

Well, the good and the bad cop from earlier would like to do something in this direction so I don't resent them for wasting half of my day too much, although it's Friday, the day I never work and always drown in whiskey, as is my ritual.

Right now, I'd do anything to pull back at least one bubble of air. Well, thinking about these two apes… Almost anything.

The door is opened by Marla, Phil's woman and the reason I'm here.

Flashback: it was Friday — therefore my day. I was at Yonder: Southern Cocktails & Brew, minding my own business and my whiskey. I was sitting at the bar so that Eryk's daughter Selina wouldn't have to walk a long way with my whiskey. Plus, I had a lovely view of her ass from here. She gave me her number once but I never called.

Suddenly Fat Phil entered the bar. I knew him vaguely. Or maybe I just read or heard something about him. He came with the two of his bodyguards. After them, Marla came in…

Yonder was one of the bars Phil had been offering "protection" to. Which meant he'd been taking their money for not demolishing them.

Eryk had a hard time, he was drowning in debt and hadn't been able to pay lately. He didn't let Phil's apes intimidate him so he invited Phil for a friendly chat.

I was sitting there, my eyes skipping from Selina's ass to Marla's reflection in the mirror behind the bar.

Phil whispered something to one of his shield bearers who immediately jumped up, stopped next to me and banged his fist against the bar. A tsunami of whiskey almost went over my tumbler's edge.

"We said three fucking PM!" he shouted at Selina. "Where's Eryk?!"

"He'll be here," she said calmly. "In a minute."

His fist landed on the bar again and at that moment the door opened and Eryk rushed in with a baseball bat. Without thinking too much, he swang the bat toward the giant at the bar, who lifted his hands to protect his head. He looked at his broken fingers in shock, tears flowing from his eyes.

Eryk headed toward Phil and hit the table with his bat. Phil fell on his ass while the other ape took a defensive stance. Marla didn't bat an eye.

I went behind Eryk's back and wrapped my arms around him.

"I'll handle this, gentlemen," I said and dragged him out.

"Jesus, Eryk, cut the bullshit!"

"Let me go, I'll kill him! I went up to my neck into debt to pay him, for fuck's sake, I can't do this anymore!"

I pushed him over to my car.

"Get in and don't do anything stupid. I'll talk to Phil."

Marla coughed behind my back.

"Phil wants a word with you," she said.

The pressure in your chest rises, your desire for air not so much. Slowly, you're getting used to it, the line between your conscious and unconscious is thinning. You don't feel the unstoppable urge to get your head above the surface anymore.

Soon after, I won Phil's trust so he "employed" me. Of course, I was responsible for the dirty little jobs that someone had to do: preparing offers to protect bars, package delivery to end consumers, liquidity assurance by breaking bones. Basically, I did a great job, decent cash for a four-day workweek — because Friday...

Then I got another interest beside whiskey. Marla. She was as cold as a spritzer and she always knew how to get what she wanted. When she focused on something, she persisted until she got it.

When Phil was on a "business trip", I was responsible to take care of her for a while. I drove her to visit Phil, took her anywhere she wanted and made sure guys kept their hands off her as he had asked me. He said nothing about my tattooed hands though.

After the second visit to jail I took her home, and when she asked me whether I'd like to stay for a whiskey or two my answer, of course, wasn't a no. A word followed a word and a drink followed a drink. All of a sudden she mounted me and by the morning we had a plan to erase Phil from our lives and pack his cash. Yup, Marla was not with Phil because she loved him or anything. She covered the "... and other entertainment activities" business area.

When your head has been underwater for so long you begin to enjoy the state of being without air. You've practically already set one foot to the other side. All it takes is just one more step. It's easier to persist. Then I hear a muffled bang and the gorilla loosens his grip. Two more — almost synchronous — bangs follow and I fall to the side with the bucket creating a big splash. I'm slowly coming back...

It has to look like a confrontation between gang members, she said. Nobody liked Phil and he had served his time more than once. And he got away with it even more times due to his connections and lawyers. My schoolmate at the police would have liked to lock him up once and for all. And if something happened to Phil the case would be closed.

Marla was occasionally scattering anonymous reports so every now and then a group of cops showed up during Phil's transactions. I never tweeted, but they had always detained me long enough to buy time to visit Phil.

Flash forward: now Phil has been out for a while and somehow he suspects that I've been passing information to the police and that something is going on between Marla and me. So he has arranged a ride to his place to have a word or two with me about ratting and love triangles. And because he isn't as content with my answers as I had been content with Marla's black triangle, I find myself in a classic scene from a black and white movie: two gorillas, a chair, a bucket full of ice-cold water and me with my hands tied behind my back.

"How far can we go?" one of the apes asks, the one who got his fingers broken on our acquaintance day.

"Very far," Phil says. "Till the end."

The apes grin.

"Hehehe," I imitate them.

The other one grabs me and dips my head into the bucket.

The air that wants to get in and the water that forces itself out make me gasp for air and cough. Someone unties my hands. I slowly pass from darkness to light without a clue what I'm going to see. But I'm pretty much aware I'm not going to like it.

The guy who once held my head underwater is now lying motionless. He's not breathing.

I sit up slowly and rub my eyes. The other one lies a couple of meters away, beside the open door. Behind my back, Marla is squirming in pain.

"No, don't die on me now, Marla!"

She smiles while blood is oozing from the corner of her mouth. She's never been so beautiful. She hands me a piece of paper with some number written on.

"Should I call someone?"

She shakes her head no.

"A code... S-safe... Phil..."

And then she's gone. I hold her for the last time. Then I stand up and head to Phil's office.

Fat Phil lies in his blood, a giant mirror behind which the safe was hidden is broken, debris all over the floor.

I check the piece of paper Marla gave me and enter the code: the future seems bright anyway...

I return to Marla, squat down and pat her head. I pull my phone from my pocket and call my schoolmate at the police. He's ecstatic and he promises not to mention me in connection with the case. He tells me to come for a beer sometime. I dial another number...

Eryk is wiping the bar and gives me a nod. Before I can say anything, a double whiskey on the rocks lands in front of me.

"Friday was yesterday, Eryk," I say and smile at him.

I put my sports bag on the bar and push it toward Eryk. He gives me a puzzled look. I take my drink and tell him to open the bag.

He grabs the bag and opens it. He's shocked. I put the empty tumbler down and wave at him.

Outside Selina is waiting for me.

"Hey, stranger! I thought you'd never call! You actually saved my number?!"

I smile at her and open the passenger door. I move the bag with the remaining half of the money to the back seat and show her to get in. I place myself behind the wheel, wink at Selina and turn the key.

HOLY FIRE

Vodka
Peppermint
Apple
Pear

There was a kindliness about intoxication — there was that indescribable gloss and glamour it gave, like the memories of ephemeral and faded evenings
— F. Scott Fitzgerald

Amounts have been left out. Live a little.

DANA KING
NOIR AT THE BAR FIGHT

"**W**hat happened there?" Stu pointed to the bandage above my left eye.

"Four stitches."

"How?"

"Got hit with a dwarf."

"A dwarf hit you? What'd he do? Stand on a chair?"

"I didn't say I got hit by a dwarf. I got hit with a dwarf."

Stu looked at me over the lip of his beer glass. "How did this happen?"

"I was over Yonder last week—"

"The night they had the fight?"

"Yep."

His resolve collapsed quicker than a snow fort in Death Valley. "You can't leave it there. Give."

I wagged my head. Shook some beer nuts in my hand. This story was worth at least three drinks.

He ordered a round and I turned my chair his direction. "The thing no one mentions is the trouble actually started at the Regulator."

"The Regulator Bookshop?"

I nodded. Wiped foam from my upper lip. "Good book stores are hard to find as virgins in a whorehouse. Everyone who came into town for the reading went over ahead of time."

"What kind of trouble starts in a book store?"

"You'd be surprised. Remember, authors make things up for a living. They don't always have the firmest grip on reality, which is why they're so willing to mess with it. Things got tense when J.D. Rhoades caught Ed Aymar putting J.D.'s books spine out so Ed could let his covers show."

"That's a big deal?"

"Damn right. People are more likely to pick up a book if the title and art work are staring at them. Spine out, your book looks pretty much like all the others."

"So what happened?"

"J.D. was cool about it. Put the books back and told Ed if he ever caught him doing anything like that again he'd sue his ass off. 'Or worse' was how he left it. He did bend back one of Ed's fingers to make the point but he didn't break it or anything. Still, blood was up even before we got to Yonder."

"I heard they had quite a crowd that night."

"You ever been to Yonder when it's packed? Not just crowded, but people so close you can smell the soap or lack thereof on the people next to you?" Stu had not. "It's something else. Ninety-nine people jammed in there ass to crotch and hot as an Amazon warehouse in July. Eryk Pruitt—you know Eryk? Him and his wife run the place— had to hold places for the readers so the guy the fire marshal planted out front with a clicker would let them in."

"Those readings—what are they called again?"

"Noir at the Bar."

"They're that popular?"

"In a cultural hotspot like Hillsborough? Damn right."

Stu noticed my smile. "What?"

"Dan Malmon. Drove all the way in from Wisconsin or Minnesota or another one of those Baja Canada states. Missed a turn in West Virginia and wound up being the hundredth person there. Prick with the clicker made him wait outside until someone else came out."

"That chickenshit. What'd Malmon do?"

"Thanked the guy for keeping him from being the one that put the crowd over and waited outside." Stu wasn't buying it. "What can I tell you? Midwestern nice."

I took my time with a swallow until Stu nudged me with his knee. "Then what?"

"I was like Number Ninety-Six, so by the time I got there Pam Stack had the remote broadcasting equipment set up and David Nemeth—he was the emcee—was already showing signs of wondering what he'd got himself into once he got a look at the crowd."

"It's a reading, for Christ's sake. How tough can the crowd be?"

I shook my head at his ignorance. "Noirs at Bars aren't like those beatnik poetry slams where everyone wears turtlenecks and berets and reads shitty poems that doesn't rhyme about how hard it is to find good vegetarian meat loaf in Iowa. This was a noir reading. People come heavy to these things."

"Bullshit."

"No shit. I bet there were more weapons in Yonder that night than the NRA sees at their headquarters in a year. Now do you want to hear the story or do you want to keep showing how little you know about writers?"

"Go ahead. I'm sorry."

"Things started out okay. Nemeth runs the hell out of these things and Pam provided commentary as each author was introduced for folks listening on the Internet. Grabs each reader as they come off the stage for a couple of quick questions while Nemeth raffles off a book. Everything's cool until Shawn Cosby gets up to read."

"Do I know him?"

"Apparently not or you'd be sure. Big guy. Works out a lot. Can bench press an F-150. Anyways, he's reading and everyone's having a ball because his stories are always worth hearing and he reads as good as he writes until he gets to a section in the point of view of a white guy who eats mayonnaise sandwiches on white bread and listens to Barry Manilow—did I mention that Shawn is black?"

"Does it matter?"

"It's about to. So he gets to that part and this dwarf in the back—wearing a MAGA hat, no less—starts yelling, 'Cultural appropriation, cultural appropriation' so's no one can hear the story and a bunch of guys in the corner join in—"

"Wait a minute. This guy's an honest to Snow White dwarf?"

"I'm not sure what the dictionary definition of dwarf is this week. Maybe he was a midget. A little person. A gnome. Fucking elf for all I know. He's about three-foot-six and built like a hydrant. He's chanting this 'cultural appropriation' shit and getting those guys in the corner worked up.

"People start getting the red ass because Shawn's telling a good story and they can't hear. It's only a matter of time before things break bad and Terri Lynn Coop broke first. She hit the sawed-off prick with a vintage 1964 GI Joe in mint condition so hard the little M-14 came loose and stuck in the guy's ear."

"What was she doing with a toy at a reading?"

"Terri's always got shit like that on her. One time at Bouchercon she stabbed a guy in the eye with a Batman Pez dispenser and damn near smothered him with a Teddy Ruxpin she had in her backpack before security pulled her off." Stu didn't believe me. "Right hand to God. I was there."

"This the same dwarf gave you the stitches?"

"How many dwarves you figure show up at these readings? It ain't like we're running Peter Dinklage film festivals. Now are you gonna let me tell the story or what?"

"Okay, sorry. Go ahead."

"This story telling is thirty work, you know."

Stu waved for two more. I wanted until money changed hands. Took a sip and gave it time achieve its destiny. "Terri hit the dwarf so hard his MAGA hat came off and everyone could see the swastika tattoo on his forehead."

"Wait a minute. A dwarf with a Nazi tattoo? In Orange County?"

"I found out later he wasn't local. Came into town with a bunch of Proud Boys who'd been sitting in the corner helping him disrupt Shawn's story."

"What were Proud Boys doing there?"

"I heard they were in town for some sort of rally at Duke. Protesting Mike Krzyzewski being Jewish or some such bullshit. Too many immigrant players on the team, maybe."

"I mean what were they doing at a reading? I know a few Proud Boys. They need Clif Notes to understand cereal boxes."

"That's the hell of it. They didn't realize they were going to s reading until it started. They saw the name of the bar—Yonder—and figured it must be a redneck joint. They about shit when they saw the slushy drink machine in the corner of the bar but they're not in the business of admitting errors or they wouldn't be white supremacists in the first place. Even Fullsteam Paycheck sounded too much like

'European Jew beer' for their taste so Eryk swallowed hard—actually, it looked like he threw up in his mouth a little—and sent out for a half-dozen of cases of PBR. That shut them up, at least until they thought Shawn was dogging them."

"Did he get to finish his story?"

"Shawn is not easily deterred. He finished his reading and went after who started the trouble. Sees the midget trying to get up and looking for who dropped him and the Proudies milling around—"

"I thought it was a dwarf."

"Prove to me you can tell a dwarf from a midget and I'll try to be more consistent. Anyways, Shawn sees Bad Santa's little helper is gunning for Terri and hauls ass back there. Picks the little fucker up by the ankles and starts swinging him around. How I got this." I pointed to the bandage on my forehead.

"Huh?" Stu said. "How?"

"Shawn got to swinging and anyone inside the radius was on his own. I didn't get out fast enough and he caught me head to head. By the time I got up the civilians were against the walls and everyone else had thrown down. David Terrenoire may not look too imposing but he has some mad martial arts skills. He went through those Proud Boys like a John Deere through a wheat field.

"Between Shawn swinging the midg—dwarf and Terrenoire wreaking havoc and Terru Lynn blinding people with Silly String things were going good for the writers. Nemeth tried to restore order for those who hadn't read yet but it was a losing battle. Pam Stack got right with the program and kept the commentary going like she was Al Michaels at the earthquake World Series game. Then one of the Proud Boys pulled a knife and cut Joe Clifford."

Stu knew Joe. "Uh-oh."

"No shit, uh-oh."

"They hurt him?"

"Not really. Sliced his arm deep enough to leave a scar on his Taylor Swift tattoo and Joe blew a gasket. Grabbed the guy who cut him, lifted him clean over his head, and threw him through the plate glass window into the street. The fire marshal waited for the guy to hit the concrete and told Malmon he could go in and—"

"Don't tell me."

"—Dan didn't get both feet across the threshold before some Proud Boy pulled a piece on Clifford and dropped Dan stiff as a two-by-four by mistake."

"Damn. That poor guy gets killed more often than Kenny."

"Once Malmon got aced Eryk decided he'd seen enough and reached behind the bar for the stash of weapons he's won at Noirs at Bars across the country. Handed me one of those ball-and-chain things knights used to carry. I was looking for a target when I heard a scream like nothing I'd ever heard before." I shuddered, not for effect. "And never want to hear again."

"What was it?"

"Sounded like a hundred little girls all got spiders dropped down their dresses at once."

"What was it?"

"I tell you it was terrible. And terrifying."

"Goddamn it, what was it?"

"Ed Aymar tried to make it out the back and ruptured his Achilles tendon."

An Achilles was one of the few body parts Stu hadn't damaged. "I hear those are painful injuries."

I shrugged. "I fought my way over there and found him on the floor curled up in a ball. I offered to help get him out but he was signing autographs for some girls and eating Cheetos he found down there and said he wanted to stay."

I showed my empty glass. Stu said, "Two more!" and threw ten dollars across the bar."

"The Proud Boys figured out pretty quick a dozen white supremacists with guns were no match for a handful or crime writers hefting medieval cutlery. They started backing their way out the door with Pam doing play-by-play all the while, careful to mention each author's newest book when describing his—or her—contribution to the mayhem. Nemeth held the door open and called them all Amazon-shopping cocksuckers as he shoved them into the street. Took about fifteen minutes to get them and all the civilians out so Eryk could lock the doors."

"How bad was the damage?"

"Property damage? I'd say a typical Thursday night at Yonder. The three dead bodies were the real problem."

"Three!?"

"Well, there was Malmon, of course."

"Of course."

"And the dwarf."

"The dwarf died?"

"Terri got that M-14 pretty deep in his ear. I thought he looked kind of unsteady when he tried to get up and I guess Shawn swinging him around like a centrifuge scrambled the little fucker's brains up pretty good." I swallowed beer.

"You said three."

I let my disgust show. "Some pain in the ass innocent bystander decided to show off for his girlfriend or boyfriend or whatever and tried to save Aymar. Went running through the dogpile just as Eryk jabbed the pike he won at Wonderland Ballroom last year at a Proud Boy and run it right through this poor bastard's eye."

I noticed Stu's suspicious look. "I didn't see any of this in the paper."

I shook my head and smiled. "Thank God for J.D. Rhoades and his J.D. I don't know what we would've done if he hadn't been there. He said he was pretty sure he could get us off on self-defense and manslaughter and the like but that juries could be unpredictable and it never hurt to dispose of bodies and go on like nothing happened."

"What'd you do with them?"

"First we had to get everyone out but Eryk and me so there'd be fewer witnesses."

"How come you two?"

"Me because I was still relatively healthy and would have no charges pending to negotiate away and Eryk because it was his joint and his pike through that guy's head. What a fucking task that was to get out."

"So what did you do?"

"Eryk waited till everyone had gone and gets me to help him move furniture so he can get the caps off the old bocce ball court. I wonder what for and he asks if I ever breathed in any of that silica dust, said it'll decompose bodies quicker'n lye. So we spent the rest of the night digging holes and filling them in, dragging those heavy goddamn caps back over the pit and putting all the furniture back like nothing happened. Wasn't till almost four-thirty when Eryk said this was good enough and I should go home and get some sleep."

"Jesus Christ."

Took me a while to start again. "I've never seen anything like looking back from the front door at Eryk standing there leaning on his shovel, tired as I've ever seen a man. Looked up at me and gave me a weird little smile. Moved his head to take in the whole room. If I live to be a hundred I'll never forget the last thing he said before

I left."

I sat remembering until Stu slapped me hard enough to knock me halfway off the stool. "What did he say?"

I reseated myself. Took a sip of beer and tried to give Stu the look Eryk gave me. "What else could he say? 'Fuck Peter Rozovsky.'"

THE FRENCH DOCTOR

Gin
Prosecco
St. Germain
Lime

"A bottle of wine contains more philosophy than
all the books in the world."
– Louis Pasteur

Amounts have been left out. Live a little.

JIM SHAFFER
TWO CLOWNS WALK INTO A BAR

That Friday evening, two men, sporting what looked like tailored Armani suits, stepped through the door of Yonder: Southern Cocktails & Brew, a hip, happenin' bar located on a busy stretch of West King Street in down town Hillsborough, North Carolina.

The royal blue suit with a subtle grey pinstripe fit the shorter, slender guy like a soft racing glove. His eye-catching, wide neon-orange tie, a carnival attraction. The taller one, broad-shouldered and thick-necked--dressed in solid black, white shirt, no tie--resembled a square chunk of headstone marble. With his knitted, caveman brow, he looked about as smart. A toothpick pinched between the short-assed bloke's painted lips bounced to the rhythm of the music. He even cut a few clumsy dance steps as he crossed the bar. The giant marble slab just shuffled in his wake.

Better than almost anyone, my bud and sometimes partner, Eryk Pruitt, the bar's owner, knew looks could be deceiving. From his spot behind the bar, he'd noticed the two visitors when they entered. They weren't regulars at Yonder, and they didn't fit, like one of those what's-wrong-with-this-picture puzzles. He turned, grabbed an emerald green bottle of Jameson off the shelf and strolled down to the end of the bar where I sat. My name's Frank Smith.

Eryk and I had known each other for a long time. Not as far back as the dinosaurs, but we two Texas-bred boys shared an affinity for the rough and tumble. I was an unlicensed investigator. To prove it, even had a small office with my name on the door right above the words UNLICENSED INVESTIGATOR. I liked to think I fixed things, made them work again. Sometimes I broke things to fix them. Whatever the shit storm, I was a regular fucking handyman. Eryk had worked with me on a couple of cases. If I needed someone trustworthy to watch my back, I called Eryk.

But with my business in a slump, we hadn't worked together for a stretch. Seemed few things needed investigating or fixing. When all was right with the world, it made me restless. So I spent most of my days at Eryk's bar, drinking to fill the empty spaces and calm my nerves. Eryk knew what I was feeling and freshened my drink from time to time. No charge.

"You see those two clowns just walked in?" Eryk asked.

I hadn't been paying attention, twisted around in my seat watching a young, dark-haired woman dance to the band's hot music. She was wearing a white summer dress, cut low and square in the front, flared, and dotted with indigo blue forget-me-nots. I watched her turn, twirl, swing her flowered hips like a pro dancer. From all angles, the dress followed her every move, but just one beat behind. She held a drink in her right hand. Didn't spill a drop. Some men watched her from the sidelines. Others broke from the pack, circled her, waiting for an invite—or an opening. I turned back towards the bar.

"She's fantastic."

Eryk glanced at the dancer. "Yeah. A real looker." He poured another inch of whiskey in my glass. "So. You know those two guys?"

I looked beyond the summer-dress dancer at the two mismatched dudes heading toward me.

"Shit. Those two clowns work for Harry Horton."

"The loan shark?"

"The same."

"What're they doin' here?"

"Lookin' for me, I expect. I owe Harry a few bucks. Stay close, Eryk."

Eryk set down the bottle and leaned up against the bar. I knew his fingers were curled around a short-handled bat hidden below the bar's surface.

"Frankie Smith." I recognized the voice behind me. The only punk I knew who called me Frankie. I didn't have to turn around, but I did. "Been looking for you, Frankie." His signature toothpick danced between his thin lips, darting from side to side like a snake smelling its prey.

"I wasn't hiding, Jerry." One of Jerry's goons stood behind him, hands clasped in front, like he was waiting for a funeral to start. Mine maybe.

Jerry was the enforcer for a loan shark named Harry Horton. I owed Harry a small sum. I didn't play cards or bet at the tables, but I did love the horses. Betting was illegal at the track in North Carolina, but online, I overfed my gluttonous habit.

My brother'd been a good friend of Harry's and a winning jockey until he got too fat for the harness. Too much booze, too many broads, too many trips to the winner's circle can go to a man's head. In my brother's case, it went to his ass. Some witty hack said it "rounded out" his career. A bright and shining one it was too, until the flame guttered and died. But while he was hot, I cashed in. I got hooked. Long after my brother's name dropped off the racing forms, I was still logging my bets. But Lady Luck had a short memory. I didn't always win. Well, that's not exactly true. The truth is, I rarely won. To cover my losses and keep my habit afloat, I borrowed from Harry. There was nothing wrong with Harry's memory. That's why Jerry and his goon stood in front of me.

"I see you brought help," I said, nodding at Jerry's goon.

"Arnold?" He glanced over his shoulder. "He's just the hired hand. He does what Harry wants him to do."

"And what does Harry want Arnold to do?"

He smiled, tilted his head to the side like an inquisitive dog. "Nothing, Frankie. This time. Not yet."

"Don't tell me Harry's getting soft." I tread carefully.

"Soft?" He struck a pensive pose, struggled to pluck an answer from the empty space between his ears. "No. More like, patient. Yeah. He's entered into the realm of patience." He lifted his arms, stretched them wide. It was a vast realm.

"Sounds like unfamiliar territory for a loan shark."

"You'd think so." He nodded, agreeing with his own statement. "But when you're king, you can do what you want. Right?" He lifted his flat palms in a questioning gesture. "I mean, I'd just as soon have Arnold here break both your legs." He shrugged. "But I'm not king."

"Lucky me. I'm grateful. Even for small things," I said.

Jerry didn't like it. He was no small thing—at least in his eyes. He took one step closer to me. His busy, pink tongue pushed the toothpick off to one side. Arnold, the goon, advanced a step. He unclasped his hands. Eryk slapped an empty hand on top of the bar. Arnold locked eyes with Eryk. I stood. Jerry's eyes never left mine. I could smell Jerry's cheap aftershave. Or maybe it was flop sweat mixed with stale cleaning fluid from his freshly pressed suit. Even an

Armani couldn't hide some stink.

Jerry was just the king's messenger boy. He knew that, but he liked it just the same. Carrying the message of doom somehow pleased him. But today there'd be no broken legs or busted jaws. He felt uncomfortable, disappointed, swimming in uncharted waters.

The toothpick stiffened between Jerry's teeth. "Harry wants to see you." His fist thudded my chest. "Now." He couldn't resist even a small dose of physical contact. "You come with us nice, or Arnold here'll escort you to the car outside."

Jerry took one step back. Arnold the enthusiastic goon advanced toward me. Eryk grabbed the green bottle of Jameson by the neck. His other hand tapped the top of the bar with the short bat that magically appeared. Meanwhile, the band still played in the other half of the bar. People still drank their cocktails and swayed to the music. Though the drinkers at our end of the bar had wisely drifted away from our little grouping, and though I could feel the pounding seismic tremor of the band's bass drum, all seemed to remain reasonably contained in Yonder world.

"Arnold. Relax," Jerry said. Arnold stutter stopped, his whole body vibrating like a mad dog's at the end of a junk yard chain. "Down boy." Jerry chuckled. "Frank's a big boy. He can walk out all by himself. Can't you, Frank? Besides, we wouldn't want to cause a scene at Eryk's bar. And you wouldn't look good with another lump on your head." Jerry laughed and waved a smart salute at Eryk.

I turned to Eryk. "No worries. If I can still hold a phone to my ear, I'll call you."

"And if you can't?"

"Smoke signals?"

Eryk kept pace with us from behind the bar as I followed Jerry out the door. Arnold, always the faithful mutt, trotted behind.

I climbed into the back of a late-model, black Cadillac, sharing the leather bench seat with Jerry. Arnold drove. The ride over to Harry's office was a short one. With Jerry and Arnold as company, it just seemed long.

They stowed me in an outer office where I watched a buxom could-be secretary filing her nails while she thumbed through a dog-eared copy of *Cosmopolitan*. No doubt looking for tips on how to become a lady once she escaped the rat race. Jerry interrupted my hopes of striking up a meaningful dialogue with the young lady when he opened Harry's office door.

"Get your ass in here, Frank."

I stood and spoke to the young secretary. "I apologize for Jerry's foul mouth."

Without lifting her eyes or missing a file stroke, she said, "That's nothing. You should hear the screams. Fucking distracting. Jerry, I'm leaving for the evening." The secretary stood and stuffed her reading material in a square Gucci bag.

"Toodle-oo, sugar." Jerry smiled and twirled his fingers at her.

Feeling like I'd just stepped into a raunchy episode of Mary Tyler Moore, I turned and strode into Harry's office.

"Sit down, Frank. Glad you could make it," Harry said. As if I had a choice. Jerry, toothpick in place, sat in a second chair to my left while Arnold posted behind me. I could feel the guard dog's hot breath on the back of my neck mixed with the odor of what I imagined was wet fur.

Harry reclined behind a solid hardwood desk that looked slightly smaller than a regulation pool table. Above, a bladed ceiling fan slowly turned, just enough to move the air. From opposing fan blades hung two model bi-planes. The revolving fan gave the illusion they were chasing one another. Harry sucked on the end of a stubby cigar while he watched them fly. He was into that World War I nostalgia shit.

He lifted his booted feet off the corner of the desk and sat forward in his captains chair, dragging it close so he could lean his elbows on the expansive desktop. He placed his smoking cigar in an emerald green ashtray nestled beside the base of an emerald-shaded bankers desk lamp. Maybe they were a matching set. On the other side of the lamp lay a cobalt blue steel gavel about the size of a stone mason's hammer, its handle finger-grooved for a better grip. The gavel rested on top of a thick stainless steel sound block, large enough to accommodate a hand. I was sure when a certain kind of justice was meted out, no hollow courtroom echo reverberated--just a scream. I thought of the secretary's words. The gavel matched nothing else on the desktop except maybe for its owner's personality. All the items sat close to Harry, within easy reach. I consciously moved my hands from the arms of the chair and dropped them out of sight below the edge of the desk.

"You owe me some money, Frank. Jerry tells me you missed your last payment."

"Business is slow, Harry."

Jerry piped up. Spit his words at me. "Why don't you get a decent job like the rest of us."

"Jerry. Take it easy. You're gonna have a coronary. I'd have to get Arnold to give you mouth to mouth." Harry snorted a laugh behind his fat cigar.

"Sure, boss." Arnold, the agreeable sort, jumped in. Jerry gave Arnold the finger.

Harry leaned back in his cushioned chair and relaxed. "I got something for you, Frank. Might help you out a bit." Jerry shifted in his chair, crossed his legs. Arnold didn't move.

"Why would you do that?" Harry wasn't the helpful type.

" 'Cause it'd help me. You have a problem with that?" He leaned forward and lifted the gavel, bounced it in his hand, testing the weight.

"Not at all."

He replaced the gavel. "Jerry tells me you're hanging out over Yonder at Eryk Pruitt's bar."

"Eryk and I go way back."

"I know. I got a job for you. And Eryk can help since he's already there."

"Doing what?"

"This ain't no deal. It's somethin' you gotta do. You see, Frank, I gotta get paid somehow."

Harry tried for a grin: pink lips stretched across jagged, yellow teeth.

"Business first. Doing the investigating? What's your day rate?" He pointed a thick finger at me. "Don't lie."

Lying hadn't crossed my mind. "Two hundred dollars."

He sat back and pondered the circling planes. "You're workin' for me now. I'll take a thousand a week off what you owe me. You'll work the weekends but I ain't payin' for them."

"For what?"

"My daughter Sylvia's got a habit of hanging out at Yonder. You keep tabs on her. Keep her outta trouble. You can't tell her anything about it. It's between us. And keep the fuckin' barflies off her. Got it?"

"I can do that."

"I'm sure you can. And get your pal Eryk to help ya. It's his bar. Don't mess this up, Frank. She's got a future. I want to see she gets there. No fuck-ups. Or I'll be sendin' Jerry and Arnold here by for a visit."

"I understand."

"I'm sure you do, Frank. You gotta still keep paying the vig every week. I can't let you off completely. You're too good a customer." Harry laughed. Jerry and Arnold laughed. I smiled."

"You have a photo. Of your daughter?"

"Sure." He opened a desk drawer and extracted what looked like a standard five by seven. He stared at it a few seconds. Following protocol, he handed it to Jerry. Jerry gave it to me. I glanced at it, then stuffed it in my pocket.

"My offer may sound generous. I hope it does. I really love my daughter. Any problems, here's my card. Call day or night." The card he placed on the edge of the desk in front of me. As he played again with the steel gavel, I snatched up the card and shoved it in my pocket. His heavy-lidded eyes held me for a still and silent moment in my chair. "Now. Get out of here, Frank. Go to work."

"Thank you," I said. Being grateful seemed the right touch, still walking and with nothing broken. I glanced at Jerry. He winked. Arnold held the door for me. Gentlemen all 'round.

I had a job. I should have been happy. But not making any money made me unhappy. One consolation though. Out on the street I pulled the photo of Harry's daughter from my pocket. Her name was Sylvia, the beautiful forget-me-not dancer.

"I can still walk," I told Eryk on the phone, "Got a job, too. Well, *we* got a job. Tell you all about it."

No chauffeur service this time, so I taxied back to Yonder.

"What you mean *we*?" Eryk asked from his spot behind the bar. He held a Jameson bottle hostage in his hand, not knowing whether he should serve me or not.

"Come on, bartender, pour. I need a drink."

Eryk reluctantly released the hostage and filled my glass. After I tossed back the shot, I relayed my little meeting with Harry. Hit the high points. Laid out the job. Played down Eryk's role.

"Look. It's my job. My responsibility. You're just here, kinda like a look-out."

"Did you mention my name?"

"I might have. I think Harry mentioned it first. Oh. Here's his card if we need to call him. Put it behind the bar." Eryk stared at the card.

"Shit. I don't like guys like Harry Horton even thinking about me. I'm in this 'cause you owe him money."

I shrugged. "Look on the bright side. I'm paying off my debt."

"The bright side. I knew I was missing something." Eryk splashed another shot in my glass.

"We all have our crosses to bear, Eryk. Cheers." I sipped the whiskey.

"Yeah. But this time I'm holding up yours, brother."

We got through the busy weekend and the following week without incident. I say we, but I just sat at the bar while Eryk did all the heavy lifting, sorting out orders, mixing drinks, keeping everyone happy, in good spirits, so to speak. I shared that good feeling: my glass constantly refilled, my debt shrinking by the day. Sylvia stopped by a few times that week. Eryk perked up when she walked through the door. Shot me a nervous glance. But with a different group of friends each time, she didn't stay long and dancing was off the menu. Outside Yonder, I didn't care what she got up to. But while she was there, I kept an eye on her, just like Harry'd asked.

Nothing happened until Saturday night.

The Yonder crowd cheered and clapped for Curtis Eller and his band who played a lively mix of foot-stomping tunes and banjo ballads. And everyone drank, keeping Eryk busy behind the bar. Sylvia appeared halfway through the evening, alone this time. She shuffled a dance step over to the bar. Stood swaying next to me. Her flowery scent drifted toward me. I couldn't place the flower. She raised her arm. Eagle-eye Eryk caught the movement, and seeing who it was standing next me, came over to take her order. He leaned over the bar.

"White Russian, please. Crushed ice?"

"You got it." Eryk shot off to mix the drink.

She caught me staring at her. She smiled.

"With crushed ice it tastes like a milkshake."

"A shake with a kick," I said. Clever me. "I saw you dancing the other night. You're good."

"Thank you. I like the music here."

"My name's Frank Smith." I extended my hand.

"Sylvia. Sylvia Horton. Pleased to meet you." She shook my hand. Eryk arrived with her drink.

"Sylvia Horton, meet Eryk Pruitt. Eryk owns Yonder." They shook.

"Nice to meet you. You got a great place here."

"Thank you. We try." Eryk even smiled. Maybe turned a little pink. Hard to tell under bar lighting.

"You aren't by any chance related to the Hortons down in Mineral Springs?" I asked.

"Don't think so. My daddy was born and raised in Hillsborough. He's got a business here. Never heard him talk about any relatives anywhere."

"What's your daddy do?"

"Something finance, I think. I don't see him much." She sipped her drink. The band kicked into gear. "Ooo. Gotta get into the groove. Nice meeting y'all."

She gave us a little wave, and with that she flitted off. I watched her go. I hoped she danced.

"You don't know any Hortons in Mineral Springs," Eryk said.

"Nope."

The band played. Sylvia danced. I watched her until a tall, dark-haired guy stepped in behind her, blocking my view. I partly stood hoping to get a better view when Sylvia spun out from behind the man. She slapped him hard in the face with her left hand, following with her right that held the White Russian. Someone screamed. I glanced behind the bar. Eryk was on the phone. I leaped out toward them. The side of the man's face streamed blood. Clumps of drinkers skittered off to the sides. Before I could reach them, the man had grabbed Sylvia and jerked her against him, his arm clenched around her neck, his hand gripping her wrist. He'd pulled a knife. Held it to the side of her neck. I looked but couldn't find Eryk. The man back pedalled toward the door, dragging Sylvia, almost lifting her off the floor. I stepped out in front of them.

"Hey. Buddy."

"What."

"You have trouble getting dates?"

"Fuck off."

Checking behind, he kept working his way toward the door. I advanced.

"Where you going?"

"None of your fucking business. Just stay back."

I held my ground when I saw Eryk step into the doorway, his

wooden bat raised. He clubbed the guy in the head hard enough to bruise an elephant. The guy's eyes rolled back. His whole body went limp. His arm fell away from Sylvia's neck. I shot forward and caught Sylvia. He fell in a heap. The knife clattered on the floor. Sylvia fell into my arms. She held on.

"What a hit," I said to Eryk. "You should try out for the majors."

Sylvia looked up at me. "Thank you."

"You should be thanking the slugger here."

Sylvia walked over and gave Eryk a hug. He should thank me. He never got that kind of attention behind the bar.

Outside I watched a black Cadillac pull to the curb. Jerry and Arnold hopped out. The back window dropped revealing Harry's pale face. Arnold dragged the guy on the floor by the ankles out to the back of the Cadillac. Popped the trunk and stuffed the guy inside. Jerry stuck his head in the door.

"Glad to see you're earning your money, Frank."

I looked at Eryk.

"I called them when it all started. Knew we'd need a clean-up crew."

"Sylvia, come here." I put my arm across her shoulders. "Go on over to the bar. I'll buy you a drink and see you get home ok tonight. Sound good?"

"Thank you, Frank. Don't know what I would've done without you both."

"Just keep dancing. You're magic," I said.

Eryk and I watched her cross to the bar. The music started again. Eryk turned to me.

"I heard this joke last week, Frank. I don't think it's very funny. But you'll probably think it's a scream. 'Two clowns walk into a bar...'"

THE BIONIC BASIL

Gin
Watermelon
Basil
Lime
Sugar

"Boo...dined on raw squirrels and any cats he could catch, that's why his hands were bloodstained—if you ate an animal raw, you could never wash the blood off."
– Harper Lee (To Kill A Mockingbird)

Amounts have been left out. Live a little.

DAVID NEMETH
RETRIBUTION

New York closed his eyes, smiled, and fell off his bar stool.
The bartender leaned over the bar and scanned the drunk for blood and bones. None, all Eryk saw was New York passed out on the barroom floor.

"Fucking New York."

Eryk's phone vibrated. Lana said that she'd be by after closing. He put his phone away and focused on the problem at hand: New York. He shook his head, turned off the music, and walked around the bar. When Eryk crouched down next to New York to check his breathing, he told the onlookers that he had him.

"You sure?" someone asked.

Another voice from behind, "You shouldn't have over-served him." Eryk turned and saw Bocce Ball, a bald guy who always paid cash and always, always complained that they covered up the bocce ball pit. Eryk couldn't remember a time when he saw Bocce Ball playing bocce ball. He didn't have the patience to deal with Bocce Ball tonight. Eryk stood and announced that Yonder was closing up early. "Sorry, y'all missed last call."

The bar echoed with sounds of a dishwasher running and New York's snoring. A bag of blue and white pills was left in the wake of Eryk dragging New York to the back of the bar. He took the bag of pills and put them behind the bar. New York was as quiet about his past as Eryk and Lana were about theirs. Closing up an hour early had certain benefits, one of which may be that he'd have New York out of the bar before Lana arrived. Eryk was cleaning out the soda guns when there was a loud knock on the front door. He turned his head front and was about to shout that they were closed, but he saw an apparition from his past, Heppy. Eryk held up a hand telling Heppy to wait. What the hell was Heppy doing in North Carolina? Eryk had put some distance between Heppy and himself; it seemed so long ago since he last ran with him. He dried his hands with the towel that rested on his shoulder. He walked to the door, his gait slowed as all the reasons he left Texas flooded back: the heat, deals gone bad, and the bodies. Thursday's sucked. The best thing about Texas was he started up with Lana. And when shit went south as it often did when he hung with Heppy, Eryk was happy she was in his corner. The towel was back over his right shoulder by the time reached the door. He unlocked it and opened it partway.

"Heppy."

"You're not going to invite me?"

Pruitt shook his head. "We're closed."

Heppy, a good foot shorter than Pruitt, slid past him and into the bar. "Not even for a friend from out of town?"

"You got the out of town part right, but you aren't a friend." Eryk closed and locked the door.

"I'm hurt," Heppy lied. He sat at one of the first stools he came to and Pruitt went behind the bar. He needed to keep his distance from Heppy, because whatever Heppy was selling, Eryk wasn't buying.

The last time he'd seen Heppy was Nacogdoches in '03.

"What the . . ." Heppy looked at the bar which seemed to be designed by Picasso during one of his opium jags.

"It allows people to sit at the bar and talk to . . . "

"Whatever." Heppy sniffed. "You gonna offer me a drink?"

"No."

"Gimme a Shiner."

"Does this look like Texas?"

"Alright, a PBR then."

"Don't carry 'em."

"No Shiner, no PBR, what kind of establishment you running here?" Heppy laughed at his own joke. With a wave of a hand, he told Eryk to surprise him. He poured a pint of brown ale and placed it in front of Heppy. He took a big swig.

Heppy looked toward the office where New York sat on the floor, his back against a wall, and his head hung down, chin against chest. "What's with him?"

"That's New York. He likes to mix his Maker's with pills." Eryk started to walk away. "I got to finish up here."

"You left Texas in a hurry."

Pruitt stopped and turned toward Heppy.

"We should have never gone to Beaumont," said Eryk.

"Potato, potahto." Heppy shrugged his shoulders and drank his beer.

Eryk hadn't thought about Beaumont for years. Lana helped them out of that one and soon he and Lana split for the Carolinas. He shook his head as if to erase those memories. Instead, he focused on unloading a dishwasher. He didn't know why Heppy was in town, but he'd find out soon enough, then he'd figure out what to do.

"Nothing like catching up with old friends," Heppy said. He put his hand to his mouth. "Oops, I'm sorry, acquaintances. Nothing like catching up with old acquaintances." Half the pint was gone.

"Those your books up there?" Heppy motioned with a nod to the books displayed above the bar.

Eryk nodded. Eryk forgot how much Heppy could talk. It's like the man couldn't stand silence.

"Can I see one?"

Eryk reached up, grabbed a book, and tossed him a copy of Townies. Heppy caught the book, flipped through it and put it to the side.

"Big-time writer. Big-time barkeep. I have to say, things are really coming up Milhouse."

Eryk picked up the floor mats and moved them to the office. Ignoring Heppy and his incessant chatter proved difficult. He came out of the office pushing a mop and bucket.

At the sight of Eryk and the mop, Heppy said, "I stand corrected." He laughed at his own joke again.

Heppy finished his beer and wiped his mouth with the back of his hand. He picked up Yonder's drink menu as Eryk mopped the floor behind the bar.

Looking at the drink menu, he said, "These signature cocktails seem fancy." He drew out the word fancy.

Eryk put the mop aside, put both hands on the bar, faced Heppy, and said, "What are you doing here?"

Heppy pulled out a Glock and put it on top of the book on the bar.

"Fantastic," said Eryk.

Heppy forced a laugh.

"I think I'll have one of those signature cocktails now." He paused a moment. "Maybe something off-menu?"

"There's no need for that," said Eryk pointing to the gun.

Heppy ignored him.

Eryk let out an audible sigh as he turned around to face the wall of bottles. Heppy and his love of guns. And Lana. Shit, Lana had no tolerance for Heppy. Gun or not, she'd rip Heppy a new one just for Beaumont. And he still had to make this prick a drink. Thursday had found a new way to suck.

Eryk remembered the pills.

"Okay, I've got something special for you." After picking up the pills, he grabbed a mortar and pestle. He crushed two blue pills and two white ones with the garlic, horseradish, and sun-dried tomatoes. He was counting on the white ones to be some sort of downer considering the state of New York; the blues, well, the blues he knew to be Viagra and adding them to the drink was just for fun. Make it three whites, he thought. He dumped the contents into a cocktail shaker filled with ice. He followed by a heavy pour of bourbon and some homemade habanero sauce. As he shook the drink, he wondered if the pills would do anything, he wondered if they'd be enough. He poured the drink into a cocktail glass, garnished it, and served.

"What do you call it?"

"The What-The-Bloody-Fuck."

Heppy laughed.

Eryk had his hands on the bar, unsure of what to do next. Heppy took a swig.

"Damn, that has a nice kick."

He took another sip.

"You're making me nervous over there. Why don't you come around and sit?"

Everything about this night had gone in the shitter from New York to Heppy and it didn't look like it was getting any better soon. As Eryk walked around the bar, Heppy pounded down the drink and, again, wiped his mouth with the back of his hand. With

Lana showing up and the possibility of all hell breaking loose, Eryk decided he'd do whatever Heppy would ask just to get him to leave.

"Damn, that was a fine drink." He put the gun back inside his jacket pocket and turned up his palms as if to say everything was all good.

Eryk stood a few feet away from Heppy.

"Why don't you pull up a stool and sit a spell," Heppy said motioning to the stool beside him. "I need to think on what's next."

Eryk thought it odd that Heppy didn't have an endgame which meant that Eryk might be able to direct the evening into his favor, though he knew it could go pear-shaped just as fast. He pulled out a stool and sat down facing the back of the building, the bar to his right, New York passed out by the office and Heppy between him and New York.

"The gun makes me nervous."

"It's supposed to."

"I figure you've got the gun to make sure I'm listening or to make sure I'm not going to get out of line. I'll be on my best behavior, Scout's Honor." Eryk held up his right hand and half-heartily flashed a Scout sign. Then an idea hit him; he had taught himself how to free himself from plastic restraints.

"There's some zip ties in the desk drawer," Eryk said. "Why don't you tie my hands up?" Eryk motioned to the office which his hands joined together the wrists. Heppy cocked his head like a dog.

"If having me tied up makes you more comfortable, then it makes me more comfortable," Eryk said. "No tricks."

Heppy nodded, mumbled something, and walked back to the office. He stood in the doorway looking at the desk and then looking back at Eryk. He repeated these quick head movements several times.

"I'm not going anywhere. Honest"

Finally, Heppy stepped in front of the desk which out of sight of Eryk. He heard a desk drawer open and close and then another one open. There was some rummaging and as Heppy appeared in the doorway, he put something in his back pocket.

"How 'bout you take off your boots and socks," said Heppy as he walked towards Eryk.

Eryk shrugged and started taking off his boots. "You mind telling me when we're going to start talking numbers?"

"Numbers?"

"Yeah, how much you looking for?"

Eryk's feet were bare and resting on the bottom rung of the bar stool. Heppy handed him a couple of ties.

"Put these around your ankles and on the stool."

Eryk tried but they were too small.

"String two together and then do it."

Eryk worked hard to make sure his hands weren't shaking but the gun and Lana were pinging around in his head. Guns always had the uncanny ability to go off when they weren't supposed to. And then there was Lana's violence. As Eryk tied his right ankle to the barstool, Heppy prepped two more ties.

"Here." Heppy hand the tie to Eryk when he looked up.

When Eryk was done with his second leg, he said okay and held out his arms. Heppy obliged.

"Money? I'm not interested in money. You couldn't afford me," Heppy said with a laugh. "No, what I'm here for is some payback."

"Payback?"

"Yeah, payback, even-out the score." Heppy walked behind the bar. "You mind?" Heppy grabbed a pint glass and filled a third with Woodford Reserve. He walked back to where Eryk was tied up and talked some more. "Payback? There's got to be a better word than that. What would one of your characters say? Revenge?"

Eryk shook his head. "Revenge has a bad Hollywood action movie written all over it. How about something like retribution?"

"Retribution?"

"Retribution has Biblical weight."

"Yeah, retribution, I like that," said Heppy. From his back pocket, he pulled out a pair a large pair of odd-looking scissors.

"What the hell ..."

"Oh these?" asked Heppy. "I think they're called chicken bone cutters."

"No," said Eryk lifting his arms and pointing a Heppy's crotch. "You're all hard and shit."

Heppy looked down at his pants.

"Man, I know you got off hurting people, but this is ..."

"Shut the fuck up!" said Heppy.

Eryk laughed. "You've got a boner."

Heppy turned around, reached into his pants, and adjusted himself. When Heppy turned and around and walked closer to Eryk, he could tell that Heppy was trying to turn on his tough-guy persona. "At first I was just going to scare you, but now, now, I'm going to hurt you."

Eryk laughed, "Oh, what are you and your boner going do?"

Heppy gulped down some bourbon. As much as he tried to be tough, Heppy would always be a Fredo.

"You ever wonder what your little toes do? Like, what's their function?"

Eryk said something about his little toe being bigger than Heppy's penis.

"Not only does the little toe help you with walking, it assists in your balance."

"Is that right, Dr Pepper?"

"Yeah, that's right. And you know what happens when you don't have your pinky toes?" Heppy didn't wait for an answer. "Your center of gravity goes off. Walking becomes hard. You have to use a cane or, worse yet, a walker. You become an old man before your time all your Little Piggies are gone for good."

Heppy stepped closer. "You should have never left."

"You went off the rails in Beaumont," said Eryk.

"I did what had to be done."

"You only did what a coked-up psycho would do."

Heppy had another belt of bourbon.

"And I learned from that," said Heppy. "No more partners, no more disappointment. I'm like Terminator 2, new and improved."

"Nah, you're the same piece of cowardly shit I've always known, but today you're a coked-up psycho with a hard-on."

"Well, this hard-on is going to fuck up your life."

For the rest of his life, Eryk would remember what he heard at that moment, it was the thud of a watermelon's hard rind cracking, but it was the sound of Heppy's skull being crushed. Heppy fell to the barroom floor, and there stood New York, unsteady on his feet and a bocce ball in his right hand.

"You alright?" asked New York.

"Yeah, yeah," said Eryk. He nodded toward the chicken bone cutter on the floor, "Could you cut me loose?"

New York dropped the bocce ball that had some of Heppy's hair stuck to it, grabbed the cutters and set Eryk free. Eryk checked Heppy for a pulse knowing that there was none.

New York padded his shirt pocket. "I believe you have something that belongs to me?"

There was something matter of fact with New York as if he'd been in situations like this before, so Eryk walked barefoot around the bar, grabbed the baggie of pills and walked him to the front door. Their goodbye was silent. Eryk locked the door. When he turned around, Lana was at the back of the bar.

"We really need to get a bell on that back door," said Eryk.

"That Heppy?" she asked pointing to the floor.

"Yeah."

"Dead?"

"Yeah."

"Saved me the trouble," she said. "I guess we've got another body to get rid of."

Lana walked behind the bar and poured herself a Redemption on the rocks. She had a sip of bourbon. "Do I even want to know how Heppy got a hard-on?"

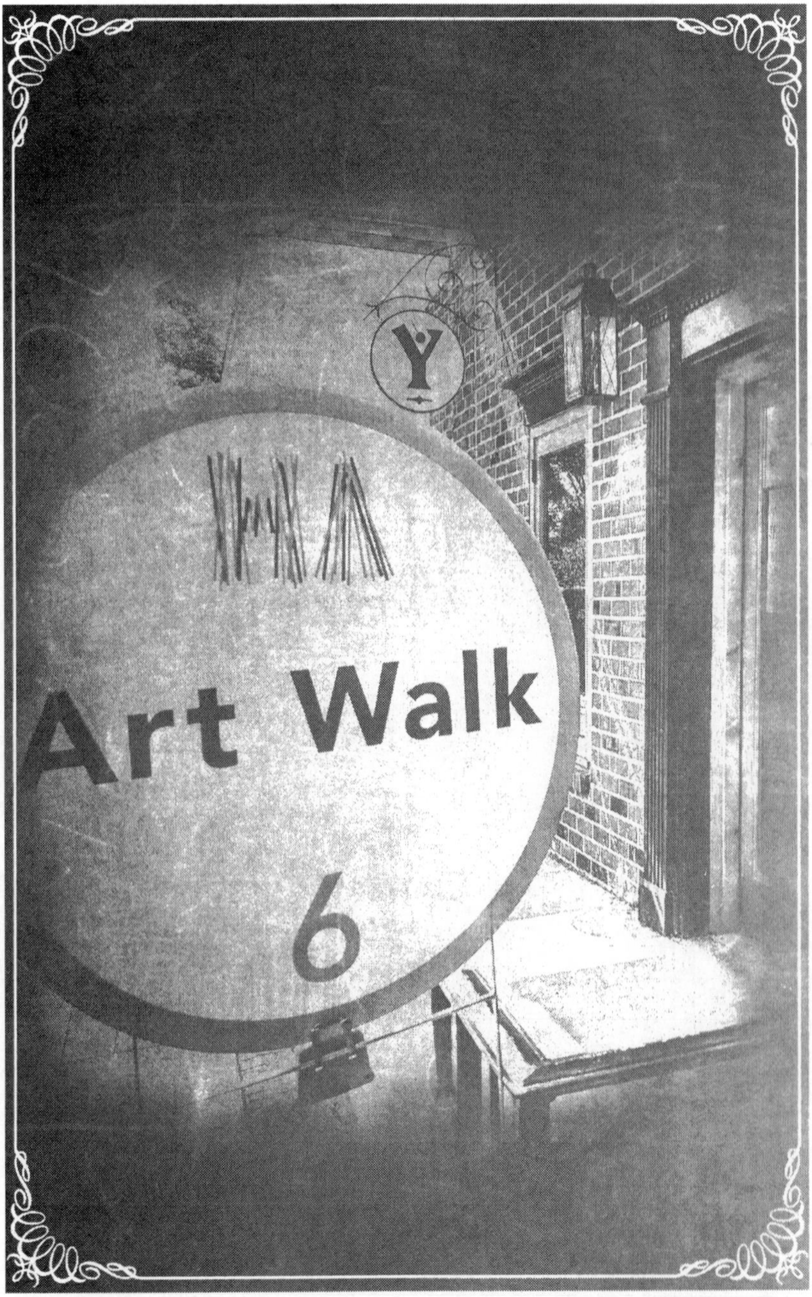
Art Walk
6

THE PEACH BELLINI

Peach Puree
Peach Schnapps
Prosecco

"Rule number one: always stick around for one more drink. That's when things happen. That's when you find out every-thing you want to know."
— John Berendt (Midnight...)

Amounts have been left out. Live a little.

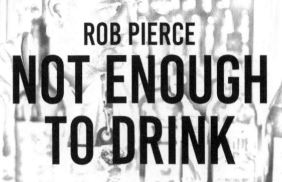

ROB PIERCE
NOT ENOUGH
TO DRINK

er face looked ten years older than her body. It all looked
hard. It all looked good. She sat on a stool at the far end
of the bar. The place was crowded and she was pretty, but
no one sat next to her. The regulars called her Hazel, although that
wasn't her name. They called her Hazel because she was nuts.

The stranger knew nothing about that, only that she looked
damned good with her legs crossed high. She had to be waiting for
someone, and not real patiently by the way she stirred the straw in
her drink. Still, there wasn't a glass or a bottle in front of the empty
stool, and he figured he might as well sit.

Hawthorne looked at the draft beers and bottles, then down the
opposite end of the bar where the bartender had a crowd to take care
of. Hawthorne settled on a beer and a shot, waved and made sure the
big man acknowledged it. He turned back, looking at the couches
and coffee tables he'd walked past to get to this stool. Strange place,
but who was he to judge? He'd been running without sleep thirty-six
hours when he saw the joint called Yonder and a parking space across
the street. He'd pulled over, tired but too wound up for coffee.

Out the corner of one eye he saw the bartender closing in, turned and ordered. Then to the woman beside him, "And what you havin, honey?"

"Name ain't honey. Everyone calls me Hazel. On account a my eyes."

Her eyes were straight up green but maybe that's what hazel was, what did he care? "What you havin', Hazel?"

"Daiquiri." She'd been ignoring her drink except to stir it. Now she took a fast sip. "You know how I like 'em, Eryk."

The big man said the price and Hawthorne pulled out his wallet, opened it wide so Hazel could see the thick wad of bills. He dropped two twenties on the bar.

"You a nice man, mister." Hazel sipped her drink fast. "Handsome men like you ain't always so nice."

No one ever mistook Hawthorne for handsome. His face was pocked, his eyes narrow and cheeks pulled in so much it was like he had meth mouth. Tiny lips and big ears and a nose that was broke more often than not. "A man'd be a fool not to be nice to a woman pretty as you."

"What do you do, uh…"

"Name's Hawthorne." He smiled, let her see the yellow teeth with gaps between. One of these days he'd get that taken care of. For now, he tested her with it.

She smiled. "What kinda name is that?"

"My grampa's. Folks call me Thorny."

Their drinks arrived and Hawthorne drank from his beer, threw back his shot. "Another!" he hollered to Eryk, who was on his way to the register with the twenties.

Hawthorne's yell was loud but his speaking voice was soft, nothing like Hazel, whose normal tone was that of a woman who'd been in bars for years and never been happy about it. A drunk for life who never thought she'd had enough. Hawthorne was fond of the type. He never stayed in any one town, could never take the chance, so he never had to deal with one for long.

He felt safe for now, that car he'd driven in recently stolen but with clean plates. A lot of cash in the trunk, but no cause for anyone to think that. Anyway, he'd tested the alarm before he bought the car and he'd hear it from the next county, much less across the street.

"Thorny?" she said. "What kinda thing is that to call a man? Makes it sound like you trouble."

"Been known to cause some." He'd let her think he was bragging, but where Hawthorne Causwell was most popular was among cops up and down the coast. They all wanted him, only in cuffs and maybe with his guts emptied out, and where'd the fun be in that? They'd lose their little chase game without him to chase, and he'd lose his money and his life. Seemed like he was doin' everyone a favor by keepin' hisself alive.

She sipped at the new daiquiri. He drank beer. The shot and his change came. At a glance he knew Eryk had already charged for the second shot. Fine, he just wanted to know how the man worked. He wasn't casing the bar, it was just a habit.

"I bet you can drink a lot," he said.

"You don't look like a slacker neither, mister. Uh, Thorny."

"No, I ain't. But there's other things I bet both of us would enjoy more."

"Don't rush me, mister. We gonna have us some drinks. Then maybe we like each other enough, maybe we dance or somethin'."

He shoulda known. She was the bar tramp, the pretty gal no one tried to take home because you could buy her drinks until closing and she might only want more drinks after that. Hawthorne could play that awhile, he'd never see this town after tonight, but he was getting laid before he left. She wouldn't just lead him on.

He stood, slid his stool so it touched hers, sat with his drinks in front of him. "No maybe about that dance," his voice smooth and soft. "We gonna drink, then we gonna slow dance." His arm was around her, his mouth almost touching hers. "To you and me, Hazel." He pulled his head away, threw back his second shot, took a drink from his beer and tightened the grip on her shoulder.

She sipped her daiquiri fast.

He drank his beer and waved. After a minute the bartender was there. Their drinks were empty. "Another beer, another daiquiri, and two more shots."

"You wanna run a tab?"

Hawthorne shook his head. "Just this round. Got places to be, might leave any time."

Like it was okay for him to drive now, much less after another round. But he'd get that car out of town before morning, however drunk he was. This gal was making it a problem was all.

The big man came back with the drinks and a slip with the total. Hawthorne opened his wallet, let the twenties drop. Today he was a rich man. Soon he'd need another job. He didn't give a fuck. He pulled jobs, he drank, he got laid. Nothing but one rush after another.

"I thought you was gonna stick around, Thorny." Her turn to talk soft, like she was gonna cry.

He pushed a shot at her. "I got this for you."

"I don't know."

"Drink it." He was sick of this bar whore bullshit. A whore who wanted more than a couple rounds commitment. Get yourself to church, girl.

Her hand shook as she reached out, brought the shot glass slowly to her lips.

Like she was a goddamn virgin.

She threw the whiskey back like she was raised on the stuff.

Hawthorne drank his, waved to the bartender with his empty glass and two fingers up. A nod in response and he drank from his beer. "Enjoy your girly drink. One more shot and we're outa here."

"No," she said, "I just wanna drink."

"You just wanna drink, don't show that much thigh. Don't be callin' me handsome like I'm stupid enough to believe it." The tone of his voice remained too low to be heard except by her. "Tell me from the start you're just drinkin' and wanna be left alone and I'll find some other whore."

"I'm not a whore." That tone like she was about to cry.

"Shut up and drink your daiquiri. We got another shot comin' then we're outa here. You wanna come back after, I won't stop ya. Only I'm goin' another direction."

The softness of her eyes was in sharp contrast to the Botoxed brow, the withered cheeks that makeup hid at a distance. She looked too young for either of those. Hell, even the soft eyes were blood-shot. Maybe her body had just held up better than her face. He sure wanted to find out.

"I took a cab here," she said. "You gonna drive me home?"

"Soon as you're ready."

"You like me, Hawthorne? I mean, not just for my looks."

"Of course, Hazel." He faked as sweet a smile as he could. "There's something deep about you. And I wanna get inside it."

She grabbed his glass and flipped the beer in his face.

He stood fast. "You little bitch."

The bartender hurried over.

Hazel stayed on her stool. "You mad at me baby?"

The bartender set their new shot glasses down. "Problem here?"

Hawthorne grabbed both shots, threw back one then the other, sat down. "Another round," he said. "Beer and a daiquiri too."

"You alright, Hazel?"

"If he ain't mad, I ain't mad."

"I'm just thirsty, that's all." Hawthorne's anger seemed to be gone. He dropped more money on the bar. He could hold back on her until they were alone.

"You mad?" she asked again.

"Never waste a good drink."

They should be out the door by now, he didn't know how well he could drive after another round, but the bitch pissed him off, he needed to calm down before he took her home. Or he might hurt her worse than he meant to.

The new round showed and he sipped his beer, didn't touch his shot right away. She'd thrown back hers when she saw how he was drinking, went back to stirring her daiquiri. Like a fight that was slow to get rolling, the opponents feeling each other out. Didn't know about her, but he needed to slow down, reduce the number of ways he wanted to pound her.

Five minutes of that, ten, and he took a good drink of his beer, threw his shot back behind it. "Let's get out of here."

His tone, his narrowed eyes, she had that daiquiri glass empty as fast as his beer.

"G'night, Eryk," she hollered across the crowded room, but it had gotten loud and he was busy.

Not that Hawthorne would have said anything anyway. He figured his tips said enough. He just wanted to get across the street with her and into the stolen car with the shotgun and ten grand in the trunk. Then to her place, fuck her and maybe slap some sense into her, like that was possible. She'd make that call, by how she was when they got there.

They stepped away from the bar, reached out for tables and chairs as they steered themselves to the door. Her place better be a short drive. They fell into each other at the exit. He pushed the door open with one hand, the other wrapped around her waist. The door fell shut behind them and his weathered hand brushed against her cheek. He pulled her to him and they kissed.

She pushed him away. "Hey! What are you doin'?"

"Just gettin' started. Don't worry, we finish at your place."

"Don't be pullin' that where my friends can see. I got a reputation."

Reputation yeah, friends he wasn't so sure.

He pointed to the black Impala across the street. "That's my car."

"Ooh, nice."

It was a 2018, nothing like the old classics, it looked like a lot of black cars out there. Which was exactly what Hawthorne wanted. Sure as hell nothing he'd call nice, but he wasn't gonna argue with pussy.

He stepped toward it but she didn't step with him. "Now what?"

"Just, there's nothin' to drink at my place. We oughta stop and get a bottle."

He shook his head and frowned. "There a store between here and your place?"

She smiled. "I know one."

This was gonna cost him a pint of whiskey but that was nothing to what a round at the bar cost, and it should be the final payment before he got what he was buying here. Renting, really, but he'd treat it like he owned it.

"Can we get it before we get in the car? I get nervous on the passenger side."

He pushed her into the street. "Just get in the fuckin' car."

She stumbled across the street and he followed, not exactly but just as awkwardly. She braced herself against the hood and made her way around, leaned against the passenger door. His own stumbling route to the driver's side was shorter. He got behind the wheel. Where he'd belonged hours before, not so much now.

She was still outside. He rolled down her window. "Get in."

"A gentleman woulda opened it for me."

"I ain't gentle." He glared.

She got in and slammed the door shut.

"Jesus."

She smiled. "There's a ABC straight down four blocks on the right. It ain't nine yet, is it?"

"Not for a couple hours. What's ABC?"

"Where we can get the hard stuff, silly."

At least they both knew what they wanted. And she'd definitely be getting the hard stuff.

He drove, dropped a hand on her thigh. She didn't say anything one way or the other. He was fine with her not talking at all.

He parked at the store and they both got out. Like she didn't trust him alone any more than he trusted her.

"Don't talk much," she said. "Don't act drunk. They ain't supposed to sell to drunks."

"Then you don't say nothin'."

He didn't need to look at her to know she didn't like that. He didn't care. She wanted the booze more than he did. He found the bourbon shelves, row after row, and almost everything by the fifth. He didn't doubt she'd drink it if he bought it. He was going to drink some of whatever they got and there were pints of Maker's Mark so he grabbed one of those, walked straight to the register and bought it, kept his mouth shut except to say "Yes, sir," when the man said the price. It was a relief to spend under twenty bucks for a change.

Outside he walked straight to the trunk, Hazel frantically following.

"What you doing with that?"

"Putting it away so you don't drink it while I drive."

He opened the trunk just a crack, didn't let her see what else was inside, set the bourbon down and shut the lid.

She slunk to her door, he walked straight like he was almost sober. She could bitch all she wanted. He wasn't taking chances on open container laws in a state he didn't know.

They weren't long on the road when she told him to turn, guided him to the dirt driveway that led a half-mile down to her little shack. It looked better than he expected, just too small to call a house. Probably fine, wasn't like anyone would stay with her more than an hour if they could help it.

"Open the door," he said. "I'll get the bottle."

She walked ahead and he opened the trunk just enough to grab the bourbon, slammed it shut. Suspicious maybe, but let her suspect away, she'd never see him after tonight.

The front door opened into her kitchen, mostly clean except for the empty wine bottles on the counters, a few empty candle holders mixed in. He took the bourbon from its bag and set it on a spare corner. She turned to face him as he pulled a knife from his coat. He cut back the bottle's wax seal, got the cap off and took a slug. Good stuff. He set his knife next to the cap on the counter and held the bottle just in front of him so she had to step close to take it. When she was done with her drink he set the bottle there too, held her in his arms and kissed her. He was drunk but he was ready.

Her arms went around him and they kissed harder, but when he pushed their bodies forward, toward where the bedroom had to be, she spun him and they reversed position.

"No," she said. "Right here." She pushed his coat off his shoulders. He obliged and it fell to the floor, then he took off his shirt and she tossed off her blouse, left her bra. "These are so good." She touched the outside of one cup. "You need to save them for last." She was taking off her skirt so he started on his pants, no mood to argue.

She pressed up against him and her tits behind the bra felt good but more than that, he was pushing into her and all this time bullshitting over drinks was worth it. Hell, he didn't care anymore, he pushed and they were moving together, back and forth, her hands on his shoulders, his on her ass. His knees were bent so the angle was right then he burst and held her tight, held them both up. He shuddered and she shuddered longer.

After a couple minutes they let each other go.

She stepped back, unhooked her bra. It fell to the floor. "Now," she said, "have a taste."

He was spent but what the hell, those tits looked good. A little good-bye kiss. His knees straight now, he knelt down and licked at one nipple, sucked on it, pressed his face tighter. And felt the slash at his throat. She pushed and he fell on his back. He tried to scream but only gurgled. He put a hand on his neck. Wet. The bitch cut him.

She stood beyond his reach, his knife in one hand as she grabbed the bourbon bottle with the other. She smiled, and he knew there was a lot of blood and it was getting worse fast and he wasn't getting up. Fucking black widow.

She drank the good bourbon, could drink it all night. She'd fucked him and he'd be dead soon, nothing to do *but* drink, for tonight anyway.

288

She'd deal with the body and the car and whatever the big secret in the trunk was tomorrow. The body would be buried out back with the others. No one ever came down here except strangers on their way out of town. Way out of town. Tonight she'd drink and relax. Tomorrow there'd be work to do.

PATRONS WHO PAID THEIR TABS

TRAVIS RICHARDSON has been a finalist and nominee for the Macavity, Anthony, and Derringer short story awards. He has 2 novellas, *Lost in Clover* and *Keeping the Record*. His short story collection, *Bloodshot and Bruised*, came out in late 2018. He couldn't be happier than to have a story set in Eryk's bar. Find more at http://www.tsrichardson.com

FRANK ZAFIRO was a police officer in Spokane, Washington, from 1993 to 2013. He retired as a captain. He is the author of numerous crime novels, including the River City novels and the Stefan Kopriva series. He is the creator and editor (and contributes to) the novella anthology series, *A Grifter's Song*, a series for which Eryk Pruitt penned the seventh episode, "Gone Dead on You." Frank lives in Redmond, Oregon, with his wife Kristi, dogs Richie and Wiley, and a very self-assured cat named Pasta. He is an avid hockey fan and a tortured guitarist.

GABRIEL VALJAN is the author of the *Roma Series* and the *Company Files* with Winter Goose Publishing. The first of five Shane Cleary novels with Level Best Books is scheduled to appear in January 2020. Gabriel lives in Boston.

WILL VIHARO is the author of The Thrillville Pulp Fiction Collection Volumes 1-3, comprising several novels including *A Mermaid Drowns in the Midnight Lounge, Freaks That Carry Your Luggage Up to the Room, Down a Dark Alley, Lavender Blonde*, and Chumpy Walnut; the "Vic Valentine, Private Eye" series starting with *Love Stories Are Too Violent For Me*; the erotic horror novella *Things I Do When I'm Awake;* and two sci-fi novels with Scott Fulks, *It Came from Hangar 18* and *The Space Needler's Intergalactic Bar Guide*, plus numerous stories in various anthologies.

TERRI LYNN COOP is a writer, recovering criminal defense attorney, and transplanted Floridian. When she's not on the beach, she's working on the adventures of Juliana Martin and Ethan Price. To read more about this disgraced lawyer and her handler-turned-lover FBI agent, check her out at Amazon or at www.terrilynncoop.com

MATT PHILLIPS lives in San Diego. His books include *Countdown, Know Me from Smoke, Accidental Outlaws, Three Kinds of Fool, Redbone,* and *The Bad Kind of Lucky.*

ERIC BEETNER is author of more than twenty novels including *All The Way Down, Rumrunners,* and *The Devil Doesn't Want Me.* He also co-hosts the Writer Types podcast and the Noir At The Bar reading series in L.A.. Visit ericbeetner.com

TODD MORR is a writer and guitarist currently living in Monument Colorado. He's published numerous short stories in places like Out of the Gutter Online and Shotgun Honey and several novels such as *Captain Cooker* (10th Rules Books) and *Instant Karma* (Fahrenheit 13).

NICK KOLAKOWSKI is the author of *Maxine Unleashes Doomsday* and *Boise Longpig Hunting Club* (both from Down & Out Books). His short fiction has appeared in Shotgun Honey, ThugLit, Plots with Guns, Mystery Tribune, and various anthologies. He prefers whiskey.

ALLISON DAVIS writes poetry (Three Rooms Press Annual Dada Magazine, Maintenant 12 and 13), short stories and is currently shopping her novel, *But Not For Me*. A background in journalism and art criticism, her day job is a senior partner at Davis Wright Tremaine LLP, a national law firm.

JUDY WILKINSON is a poetess who enjoys the finer things in life, such as drinking boxed wine, making questionable choices, and writing stories in hopes of either scaring people, or making them cry. She currently lives in Hillsborough, NC along with her three cats, Pepper, Gracie, and Lucifer.

S.A. COSBY is an Anthony-nominated writer and miscreant from southeastern Virginia. His work has appeared in numerous magazines and anthologies...his novels include *My Darkest Prayer* from Intrigue Publishing and *Blacktop Wasteland* coming in 2020 from Flatiron Books. In his spare time he enjoys chess and social upheaval.

PHILIP KIMBROUGH - After growing up in Greensboro, N.C., Philip Kimbrough graduated from Elon University with a film studies degree and promptly took a short, two-year vacation in Los Angeles. Today, he lives in Hillsborough, N.C., with his wife, Meagan, and their dog, Lucy. *The Proposition* is his first published piece.

STACIE A. LEININGER is an avid writer who received her English Degree from The College of St. Rose in 2002. She has won multiple awards, for her literary works, since her first published piece at age 9. Her favorite genres are Science Fiction, Crime, comedy, and poetry.

GREG HERREN is an award winning author/ editor from New Orleans. His short story collection *Survivor's Guilt and Other Stories* was published in April 2019; his novel *Royal Street Reveillon* was released in September 2019.

BRUCE ROBERT COFFIN is the bestselling author of the Detective Byron mysteries. His most recent novel, *Beyond the Truth,* was a finalist for the Agatha Award, the Maine Literary Award, and winner of the Silver Falchion Award for Best Procedural. His short fiction appears in several anthologies, including *Best American Mystery Stories 2016.*

RENATO BRATOVIĆ is an advertising creative and writer from Slovenia. He writes in Slovene (his mother tongue, of course, he does) and in English (a bridge to global readers). His third short story collection is on its way. His stories appeared in Noir Nation 3, Exiles: An Outsider Anthology, BalkaNoir...

DANA KING's Nick Forte Private Eye series has earned two Shamus Award nominations from the Private Eye Writers of America. He also writes the Penns River procedural novels. Dana is published by Down & Out Books. You can learn more about Dana at his web site www.danakingauthor.com.

JAMES SHAFFER is the author of the novella *Back to the World* (Close to the Bone). His crime fiction stories have appeared in anthologies and on line at Close to the Bone, Flash Fiction Offensive, Retreats From Oblivion, and Punk Noir Magazine. He's on Facebook at: Jim Shaffer.

DAVID NEMETH lives in Wilmington, Delaware with his wife, son, and two dogs. He is a graduate of Emerson College with a BFA in Creative Writing. He is the editor of Unlawful Acts, a columnist at Do Some Damage and has written for The Thrill Begins. His fiction has appeared in Shotgun Honey and Flash Fiction Offensive. His poetry has appeared in Lost & Found Times, Mudfish, Old Red Kimono, and Spore 2.0. He was also in The First Hay(Na)Ku Anthology.

ROB PIERCE wrote the novels *Tommy Shakes* (Sept. 2019), *Uncle Dust*, and *With The Right Enemies*, the novella *Vern In The Heat*, and the short story collection *The Things I Love Will Kill Me Yet*. He lives and will probably die in Oakland, California.

THE BARTENDER

ERYK PRUITT is a screenwriter, author, and filmmaker living in Durham, NC. His films "Foodie" and "Going Down Slow" have won awards at festivals across the country. His fiction has been nominated for both the Derringer and the Anthony awards. His novels include *Dirtbags, Hashtag,* and *What We Reckon,* and his short fiction has been collected in Townies. He is the co-host of the true crime podcast The Long Dance. A full list of his credits can be found at www.erykpruitt.com

THE BARBACK

LIAM SWEENY is a writer, editor, and disaster worker from upstate New York. He is the author of the "Jack LeClere" detective series, and is the Editor-in-Chief/Creative Director of Xperience, a Capital Region, NY music, art and culture publication.

LIVE MUSIC

DAN BARBOUR - Born and raised in Durham NC, Dan Barbour co-founded Ellerbe Creek Band in 2008. His many experiences with music and the relationships that have come with it have given him a lifetime of stories to be told.

Made in the USA
Columbia, SC
02 January 2020